Raised as a Goon 2

Lock Down Publications and Ca$h Presents
Raised as a Goon 2
A Novel by *Ghost*

Lock Down Publications
P.O. Box 1482
Pine Lake, Ga 30072-1482

Lock Down Publications
Like our page on Facebook: Lock Down Publications @
www.facebook.com/lockdownpublications.ldp
Cover design and layout by: **Dynasty Cover Me**
Book interior design by: **Shawn Walker**
Edited by: **Mia Rucker**

Stay Connected with Us!

Text **LOCKDOWN** to 22828 to stay up-to-date with new releases, sneak peaks, contests and more...

Thank you!

Submission Guideline.

Submit the first three chapters of your completed manuscript to ldpsubmissions@gmail.com, subject line: Your book's title. The manuscript must be in a .doc file and sent as an attachment. Document should be in Times New Roman, double spaced and in size 12 font. Also, provide your synopsis and full contact information. If sending multiple submissions, they must each be in a separate email.

Have a story but no way to send it electronically? You can still submit to LDP/Ca$h Presents. Send in the first three chapters, written or typed, of your completed manuscript to:

LDP: Submissions Dept
Po Box 1482
Pine Lake, Ga 30072

DO NOT send original manuscript. Must be a duplicate.

Provide your synopsis and a cover letter containing your full contact information.

Thanks for considering LDP and Ca$h Presents.

Dedications

This book is dedicated to my perfect Baby Girl born March 10th. As long as I'm breathing, you'll never need nor want for anything. The world is yours.

Acknowledgements

Gotta send my love to my big homie, **Ca$h**, for giving me the opportunity to put them birds down. You showing me another way, and for that reason I honor you to the utmost. I know I came to the label with a lot of baggage because of that Dope Boy lifestyle I'm trying to leave alone, but you giving me my chance-now we eating.

Shawn, you so one hunnit. I sent a lil portion of my manuscript to you just trying some shit and you told me I had talent and needed to focus on that, and leave that old lifestyle alone. Thank you, sis. I love you. Just know I got you.

Mad love ot the rest of the LDP Family. **The Game Is OURS.**

Note To Readers:

Before I released this part 2 to the world, I had allowed my Moms to read it just to be sure that she'd be okay with the uncuts that were revealed in here, in regards to our situation. At first, I had watered it down so it wouln't be so raw. She didn't like it.

Her exact words were, *"Son, ain't nothing phoney about you or me. I want you to present this story to the world exactly how it happened and fuck their judgement. In order for them to understand who you are as a writer, they must embrace the TRUE you."*

And I agree, so, with that being said, here's part 2. Based on real life events.

Chapter 1

My brother pumped the shotgun and put it back inside of my mouth. "I ain't never felt like you were my brother anyway. Die, nigga!" I saw him place his forefinger on the trigger, preparing to end me.

With one swift motion, I smacked the barrel away from my mouth.

Boom!

Came a loud blast, sending a burning sensation through my upper right shoulder, making me feel as though I had been stabbed with a flaming sword. My arm went limp and I would have sworn that the nigga knocked my arm off altogether. A tear crept in the corner of my eyes from the impact.

This nigga really want me dead.

Reality was a muthafucka. Crazy how my own blood would do me. I felt betrayed, somewhat afraid, but knew what had to be done.

Before he could pump his gun again to fire another shot, I bounced off the bed, tackling him into the dresser, causing the shotgun to fall out of his hands and onto the floor. We tussled against one another, both huffing and puffing, while the constant reminder of my pained shoulder, never left my mind.

"Get off me, bitch nigga, I gotta kill you like Juice said or he gon' kill me!"

He crashed my back against the dresser with so much force that the mirror shattered, spewing glass everywhere and the dresser handle hung off its hinges.

"Ahhh, fuck!" The nail from the broken dresser handle pierced the same shoulder I had been shot in.

Gotto knelt down to grab the shotgun. Seeing my chance, I yanked him by the back of his head and brought my knee up to his face.

Crack!

Spurts of his blood coated my kneecap like hot ketchup.

"Arrgggh!" He wailed out in obvious pain.

Furiously, I lifted my knee up to meet his face once again.

Crack!

I felt his nose break from the impact. Staggering to get to his feet, he grabbed me up into the air, shocking the shit out of me and slammed me onto the bed. I don't know where he had got the strength from, but he had me pinned to the mattress. I couldn't for the life of me, get from under him.

"I gotta do what I gotta do, bro. Pops said Juice in charge." He bounced off of me and dove to the floor in pursuit of the shotgun.

The shotgun was no less than five feet away from us. Using my last bit of strength, I lunged forward and snatched up the gun up, aiming it in his direction. My heartbeat sped up rapidly. Adrenaline shot through me as Gotto ran face first into the barrel.

Boom!

Everything happened in slow motion. The bullet left the gun, cracking through the air as loud as thunder, punching a massive whole through his face. Blood and brain matter splattered from his head unto the wall, before he fell to the floor, with his left leg jerking.

I stood over him as hatred for him and Juice took over my body. He was no longer my brother. He was the enemy. A demon spawn of my father, who I hated more than anything. I cocked the shotgun, placing the barrel to his chest, right over his heart.

"Rest in peace, fuck nigga!"

Boom!

His body leaped from the pavement, landing him on his side as a pool of blood surrounded him, and his spinal cord hung from his back.

That was the same story I told my guy, Tywain, as we chopped up Gotto's body, preparing to dispose of the remains.

Two days after I had had my surgery, he had come to my house to help me get rid of Gotto.. We had threw his body into a metal garbage can where we doused him with gasoline, and set him on fire. Watching his body burn and sizzle, I felt absolutely nothing. My oldest brother, Juice, had sent him to kill me because he'd thought I had him locked up for no reason.

The reality of that situation was that Juice had kidnapped the daughter of a very wealthy and powerful Russian, who had so much pull that he could order the hit for my entire family, and have those orders carried out in less than twenty-four hours. That hit would include taking the lives of my mother and my little sister, who were both innocent in all of this.

Juice's right hand man, Pac Man had already killed the powerful Russian's son, and afterwards, Juice killed him. . Had Juice stayed on the streets and tried to carry out his plan of holding the powerful Russian's daughter for ransom, there would have been an all-out war waged. Serge had a strong hand that reached all the way back to Russia. He was a man well connected and deeply rooted within the underworld, as well as the political world. My brother didn't know what he was getting himself into. He had been so doped up on heroin for the last few weeks that his mind had been extremely clouded.

Prior to his arrest, some of his old enemies had shot up my mother's house. In the process, they had managed to miss him and hit an innocent woman that we grew up calling our aunty. She'd gotten shot in the back. Directly after her surgery, the detectives questioned her, and a few days later, I had her tell them that my brother was the target so that they could pick him up for questioning. I needed to get him off of the streets because he had Serge's daughter chained up in our basement.

After his arrest, I freed her, and made a deal with her and her father. I didn't know how long it would be before that deal was broken, or it was found out that Juice had been the one to kidnap her in the first place. But Nastia assured me that she would keep the secret.

Tywain helped me to change the gauze and patches on my shoulder. "Bro, I swear, you got the craziest family that I've ever seen. I mean, your own brother tried to knock your noodles out." He shook his head as he taped me up.

"Yeah, well you see how that worked out for him. That nigga, Juice, must've been all in his head." I slid my wife-beater over my head and down my body. I rotated my shoulder a little bit, wincing in pain.

Tywain laughed. "Bro, you actin' like you got your arm knocked off. All he did was severely graze you. You lucky, I hope you know that." He turned his back and walked out of the bathroom. I followed close behind.

"Fuck you, let me see you get hit by a shotgun shell, and then you tell me how you'd act." I wasn't trying to hear what he was talking about because my shoulder was killing me and I wasn't for taking no pain medication or nothing like that. I didn't want to put nothing into my body that I would get addicted to.

Tywain stepped in the living room of my mother's house, taking his shirt off. "Nigga, you wanna see some war wounds? Look at all these. I been shot fourteen times. That's the same amount of times that Tupac and Fifty Cent got shot combined." He started pointing to the wounds all over his upper body. "This one right here," he said, pointing to his stomach wounds. "I got popped by a Nine in my stomach when I was twelve years old. That was the same summer I got a .380 and kilt my first nigga. It's like after you catch that first hot one, it turn you into a savage 'cuz you no longer wanna be on that receivin' end. I killed three niggas that summer, and got popped here and here that winter," he said, pointing to two other bullet wounds in his shoulder and chest. Before it was all said and done, he'd shown me all of his war wounds and told me the story behind them.

After listening to him, and hearing how young he was when he first got shot, it made my situation not seem so bad. I mean, my shoulder still hurt like hell, but I knew it would get better. We bleached the entire bedroom from ceiling to floor, and then sprayed the blue spray all over the room that highlighted any blood splatter.

After doing this three times, until it came back thoroughly spotless, we put our kits away and loaded them into his truck. We had already poured my brothers bones into the lake, after smashing them in a bag with a sledge hammer until they turned to dust. I was no rookie at getting rid of a body.

My father was a savage of a man. I'd watched him kill more than a few people, and he always took me and my older brother along when he disposed of the bodies in one way or the other. As I was walking outside to get into Tywain's truck, Shakia called my name from her back window.

It took everything in me not to ignore her ass because less than a week ago, I'd caught her fucking my little brother, Gotto on our living room floor, even though she was supposed to be pregnant by me. Her mother, Shaneeta, had been shot in the back. She had been the one who took my virginity when I was only fourteen years old. I paused in place, and put my hand over my shoulder.

"What up, Shakia?" I asked, turning around to face her backyard.

"I'm about to come outside 'cuz I need to holler at you for a minute. Can you at least grant me that?" she asked with tears in her eyes.

I waved her outside. I really didn't feel like talking to her, but she did stay right next door. I needed to see if there was anything suspicious in her demeanor. That would tell me if she had heard anything the night before when I killed Gotto.

"Alright, hold on." She looked excited that she would finally be able to have my ear.

Tywain came out of my mother's house with a juice in his hand. He looked like he was losing weight. He was already skinny, and damn near six feet five inches tall. He had on a wife beater that barely hung to him. I don't think fighting was his thing because he was so small, but he definitely kept them *hammers* with him. In that moment, he had a fat ass .45 in the small of his back.

"Yo, let's go check on the traps, kid. It's been a few days and we got hella bread to snatch up."

Shakia came out the side door of her house that led into our backyard. As soon as Tywain saw her, he rolled his eyes. She caught him, and stopped, placing her hand on her hip.

"Excuse you, but what you rolling your eyes for, like you a female or something?"

Tywain curled his lip, looking at her like he was disgusted. "Look, Shakia, I don't fuck with loud mouth ass females. I'll knock a bitch out wit no hesitation, so I'd advise you to keep yo ass movin' before yo face meet the ground. Word is bond." He flared his nostrils.

She looked like she was completely offended. She looked from him to me. "Damn, Taurus, you gon' let him talk to me like that?"

I shrugged my shoulders. "That shit ain't got nothing to do with me. The man said to leave him alone, maybe that's in your best interest."

She looked at me for a long time before walking closer. "I mean, even if you are salty at me because of what happened between me and your brother, I'm still the mother of your child. That gotta count for something."

"That shit ain't no guarantee," I said, giving her a look like she was crazy.

"Wait a fuckin' minute. What you mean by that?" she questioned, getting in my personal space.

I took a step back and moved her out of my face. "Come on now, Shakia. I ain't finna do all this dumb childish shit. You know what I mean. If you 'a fuck my blood brother on my mother's living room floor, right after I saved your life, then ain't no telling who that baby's daddy is."

She blinked tears and swallowed. "I made one mistake. One fuckin' mistake, at a vulnerable time, and now you frontin' like you ain't take my virginity, and this baby ain't yours." She took a deep breath, her bottom lip quivering. "That was the first time I'd ever did anything. The first and the last time. I ain't said a word to your brother ever since that day." She looked toward the sky as tears escaped the corners of her eyes. "I know I made a mistake, but don't let that be the reason you give up on our child before it even gets here, because that's not fair at all."

I didn't know what to say to her at that time. It didn't seem to me that she knew about what happened to my brother, or at least she put on a good front like she wasn't aware of anything. Either way, I was done talking to her. It was starting to get hot outside and it was too early to be arguing with a female. "I don't want to get into all of that. How's your mother doin'?"

She frowned. "Damn, all you care about is her. I'm sittin' here tryna find out if everything between us will be okay, and you're too busy worried about my mother. We have a whole ass baby on the way. What part of that don't you understand?"

Tywain waved her off. "Bro, let's go. She ain't talking 'bout shit." He shook his head in annoyance.

She turned around and got into his face. "You know what, Tywain, I don't give a fuck if you got a gun on you or not. I'm not scared of you. You better stop speakin' on me before we be out here fightin'. Now say somethin' else on my name and see what I do."

Before I could get between them, Tywain looked over her shoulder at me, raised his hand and smacked her so hard that it echoed. She yelped and fell to the ground holding her face.

"Bitch, I told you to stop playin' wit me. I ain't one of these lame ass niggas on the street. I'll kill yo ass, quick!"

I ran to her side, picking her up off of the ground. She was crying like a baby. "He didn't have to do me like that. Why did you let him do that, Taurus? I'm the mother of your child."

I tried to calm her down. "Shakia, just chill out sometimes. You can't be runnin' up in everybody face and not expect them to do somethin' to you. That ain't cool."

She jerked out of my embrace. "This nigga put his hands on me and you make it seem like it's my fault. What type of shit is that?" She looked angry, and a little hurt. "You use to never even let nobody talk to me wrong. Now you lettin' niggas beat my ass and shit. I don't know why you blowin' me fuckin' your brother one time, out of proportion. You been fuckin' my mother since day one, and I never held that against you, and I know y'all was fuckin' while we were together. So how much of a hypocrite can you be?"

"Let's go, kid. It's too early for all this drama and shit. It's plenty hoes out here. Shakia ain't even all that."

Shakia spun around to face him. "Oh, now I'm not all that, but you the same muthafucka that tried to get at me when I was just in the eighth grade. Since I ain't give you no play, but gave yo mans the pussy, you wanna put your hands on me now? That make you feel vindicated?" She rolled her eyes. "You lucky I ain't got no brothers, because if I did, they'd be fuckin' you up right now."

Tywain walked past her and bumped her. "Yeah, whatever, bitch. Trust me, if you did have some brothers and they tried me, or talked to me like you doin' right now, shit a be fucked up for your family. Word is bond." He opened the door to his car that was parked in the alley.

"Yo, end this conversation, and let's rollout, Taurus. This broad givin' me a headache." He closed the door and I could see him messing with the controls on his dashboard.

I turned to Shakia. "Look, until I find out if that's my child or not, I'm gon' do my best to make sure you stay straight on all levels. Financially, I got you. I just ain't fuckin' wit you right now. I gotta clear my head and get myself together. I ain't tripping' over the you screwin' Gotto thing no more 'cuz we wasn't together, and we never will be. You do whatever and whoever you wanna do. It ain't for me to say shit about it," I stated calmly as I swatted a fly out of my face. "I'll be at the next doctor's appointment, and every one after that." I walked off.

She ran in front of me and dropped to her knees. "Please don't do me like that, Taurus. I need you, baby. I can't handle this shit on my own. She wrapped her arms around my legs, almost causing me to fall over.

I was feeling some type of way. I wasn't trying to flex on her or nothing like that, and I genuinely cared for her, but I felt like she betrayed me by fucking my brother. Her bringing up the fact that me and her mother was messing around was irrelevant because she knew about our relationship before she gave me the pussy. The fact of the matter was, her and I weren't together, but at the same time I felt like she was doing some dirty shit behind my back, and I didn't like sneaky people. If I couldn't trust you, then I didn't fuck with you. It was as simple as that. I pulled her up by her arms and pulled her into my embrace.

"Shakia, get a hold of yourself. We'll talk about all of this later. Let's just take some time to calm down so we can get a better grip on things." I kissed her on the forehead.

She melted into my lips and tried to wrap her arms around me, but I stopped her by blocking her hands. I could feel her body immediately get weak. She lowered her head and walked away from me without saying another word.

Chapter 2

I went to see Juice in the county jail. I felt like it was my place to let him know the reason I had did what I did. I didn't want there to be any bad blood between me and him. My brother was a hot head. He had the same temper as my father, but probably less feelings. He didn't give a fuck about nobody. I think he barely even cared about himself, and after he started doing heroin, he became ten times worse. I felt that if I went to see him and explained to him my side of things, hopefully he would see things my way, and we could move past the whole ordeal.

When I got to the booth where the phone and bulletproof glass was, Juice was already seated on the other side of the glass. His face was frowned into a scowl, and he had both of his fists balled up.

As soon as I sat down, he grabbed the phone off of the hook on the other side with so much aggression that he damn near ripped it off of the wall. He started yelling into it but I couldn't hear him because I hadn't picked up my phone yet. He smacked the glass with his hand and pointed to my phone. I picked it up and put it to my ear.

"Bitch ass nigga, how you gon' have this punk ass bitch set me up like that?" he snarled.

I held up a hand to him. "Nigga, you need to calm down 'cause you don't know what you had gotten yourself into. I-"

Before I could finish what I had say, he cut me off, punching the glass.

"I don't give a fuck what I was gettin' myself into. You don't have some off-brand ass bitch get me locked up. I'm yo big brother. Pops put me in charge, so if anything, you supposed to be doin' what the fuck I say and not the other way around. Don't you know I'm sick in this muhfucka? I been throwin' up 'n shit since I been here, and my body hurt." He wrapped his arms around himself.

"You only gon' be in here for a few weeks. I just needed to have you sit down in here so I could let you know what was goin' on because you wasn't tryna listen to me out there."

He moved his face closer to the window. "So, you get me locked up? What type of ho shit is that? Since when we start playin' fuck nigga games?"

I dismissed his comments. "Bro, that broad you snatched up wasn't no average female. Her people super plugged."

He shrugged his shoulders. "I don't give no fuck. Fuck her people, nigga, and fuck you for getting me locked up for this bitch."

"If you shut the fuck up and let me finish, because you was so doped up out here that you was makin' stupid decisions, decisions that was gon' get our mother and little sister killed, along with ourselves. Now what I'm tellin' you is that this chick people plugged all up in Russia. Her father got influence like you'll never believe. All it would have took was for him to find out that you was the one that had his kids, and not only would he have murdered you to get them back, but he would have wiped out our entire bloodline."

Juice curled his lip. "What's this muhfucka name?"

I shook my head, "Never mind that. The point is that if I wouldn't have stopped all of that shit, we would have been knocked off by these white muhfuckas. I did what I had to."

"What's his name?"

"That shit ain't important."

He punched the glass and stood up. "Fuck nigga, you got me handcuffed in this muhfucka, locked away from freedom, and you tellin' me that it ain't important!" He took a deep breath. "Bro, if you don't tell me this nigga name, I swear to god, I'mma find a way to body yo ass." His chest was heaving up and down as if he were out of breath. "Now, what's his name?"

His threats weren't getting to me. I didn't fear my brother. I knew that if it came down to it, I could out think him. He was impulsive. Majority of the things he did were on the whim, whereas I was extremely calculating. I really didn't see the need to keep Serge's name from him at that time, but now looking back, I wish I would have. "His name is Serge, and the daughter you held captive, her name is Nastia. The dude Pac Man killed was his son."

He nodded his head, curling the right side of his lip slowly. "Well you tell Serge that I don't give a fuck about him or his punk ass daughter. If it was up to me, after I fucked that pink bitch, I would have blown her brains out. Tell him that he lucky he got a house nigga like you to trade in one of their own for the sake of his, because I would have never done that for no amount of money." He looked down and then straight into my eyes. "When I get outta this muhfucka, I'm killing you, Taurus. If I can whack yo punk ass before I get out, that'll be even better. But on my first day out, you will be my number one priority. That's my word." He spit a greenish-yellow loogey on the glass. "You a dead nigga. My father was right." He threw the phone against the window and called the guard.

As I was leaving out of the jail, something in me clicked and I got it. I had made my mind up that it was time for me to get a little crazier and a lot more hood.

Muhfuckas wasn't honoring my humbleness. They took that shit as a sign of weakness. My heart had to become as cold as an ice box, with ice water running through my veins. I knew that I had to slay this nigga just like I did Gotto. That bro shit was out the window. I had to wait until the right time, but 'til then, I had to play my cards just right.

Two months had passed before I got a call from Serge's daughter saying that she wanted to sit down and have dinner so we could come to an understanding about things.

I was at the doctor's office with Shakia when I received the call. I told her that we could meet up that night, and she said she'd pick me up, to which I agreed.

Later that night, Nastia met me at the BP gas station around the corner from my house. She pulled up in an all pink and black Aston Martin. When the car stopped in front of me and the window rolled down, my first thought was that it was a hit and I almost reached for my Glock .9.

Before I could reach for it, I saw her smiling face appear. She waved and popped the lock to her passenger's door. I got in. Her car smelled of Jasmine. The seats were all leather, and extremely comfortable. I felt a little uneasy at first. I mean, my people had killed her brother and kidnapped her, so I really didn't know what to say, or why she wanted to meet up with me. I sat quiet in my seat for a long time.

She reached over and patted my thigh. "Your name is Taurus, right?" she asked, looking over at me with a warm smile on her face.

"Yeah."

"Well, Taurus, I don't want you to feel uncomfortable with me because you saved my life, and I owe it to you. I just thought you should know that." She squeezed my thigh, and flipped her long blonde hair over her shoulders.

I had to admit that she cleaned up nice. She looked like a completely different female now that she had been able to get herself together. I was impressed. I still felt somewhat nervous. I had never been alone around a white girl before. It felt weird, especially since my mother raised me to stay away from them. She always said that they were nothing but trouble.

"Nastia, you know you don't have to keep sayin' that. My brother had got caught up on the wrong move, and I couldn't let him go out like that. If I could have saved your brother, I would have. I just got there way too late."

She waved me off. "Forget about him. He was dead weight. Sooner or later, he would have been killed anyway. You can be sure of that." Her cellphone vibrated. She looked at the face, and then ignored it, placing it back into her lap. "I don't deal in weaknesses. My brother was a wimp. He was more emotional than me, and I could not depend on him for anything of substance." She rubbed her hand up and down my thigh again. "You see, I have a vision in mind that only a strong man can bring into fruition, a strong black man like you."

I know the look on my face spoke volumes. I was so confused, and I didn't know what to think, or even how to feel. With every word that came out of her mouth, I grew more confused.

Seeing my face, she laughed out loud. "Don't you worry yourself, baby. You'll understand everything in time."

We went to a five-star restaurant called Dimaggio's. It was located on the suburban side of town where the upper crust of society resided. I'm talking judges, senators, chemical engineers, and people of that sort.

Her car was valeted, and we stepped into the dimly lit restaurant with her arm inside of mine. It felt weird to be walking with a white girl like that. It felt like all eyes were on us, and they probably were. It didn't take long for us to be seated at a nice table, way in the back of the establishment.

She gave a finely dressed man our orders, and smiled at me. "You look so tense. Are you always this way?" she asked as a bottle of white wine was placed onto the table. I watched her pour herself a glass, before pouring me some as well.

I rolled my head around on my shoulders. I had to snap out of whatever mood I was in because I couldn't think clearly. I tried to live life everyday as if it were a chess match. I had to think that Nastia was setting up her pieces with a strategy in mind, and if I didn't pay close attention, I would sleep on her first moves, and that could wind up being deadly for me. So I mentally calmed myself down, and smiled.

"Nall, it's just this atmosphere is a little fresh to me. I feel out of place."

She reached across the table and touched my hand. "It's okay. You're going to get used to things like this, if I have anything to do with it." I felt her curl her fingers into mine.

The waiter came and placed nice elegant plates of New York strip steaks before us. I was so hungry that I dived into my food like a beast, while she ate all prim and proper with her fork and knife. I ain't have time for all that. I picked that bad boy up with my fork and ripped it apart with my teeth. I had my steak well done, so it was extra good to me.

"Taurus, the reason I wanted to bring you out tonight is because I am really thankful for you. No matter how much you try and downplay things, if you had not come along when you did, I would have been dead, or severely hurt. So for you rescuing me, and coming to my aid, I am in your debt. I will do anything for you, as long as you allow me to." She touched my hand and trailed her fingers over the top of it. "So what can I do for you?"

I wiped my mouth with the big thick towel-like napkin. I was full as hell. I took a sip of the wine, swishing it around in my mouth before swallowing it altogether. I was trying to buy time to see if I could see where she was coming from. I felt like she was being too nice, and that comment about her brother was still getting to me. "Before we discuss all of that, Nastia, why don't you tell me a little about yourself so that I can get to know you better?"

She lifted my hand and kissed two of my fingers, sucking the juice of the steak off of them, looking me straight in the eye the whole time. "First things first, I love your skin complexion. I love your race of people. I love your culture, and there is something about you that drives me completely insane." She straightened up in her seat when the waiter came over and asked us if we wanted dessert, to which we both declined.

I took another sip of the wine and swished it around my mouth. The flavor was rich. It was the first time in my life that I had actually tried it, and I liked it. I swallowed another gulp full before responding. "Tell me about your brother, and why his death doesn't really bother you."

She held up a finger and wagged it at me in a disciplining fashion. "I didn't say his death didn't bother me. I said, at the rate that he was going, he would have wound up being killed sooner than later anyway. Me and my brother were close, but I had no faith in him when it came to business matters. All he cared about were little girls. He was the worst kind of pedophile that you would ever meet. He ordered kids from different countries just so he could molest them, and they were never older than five. He got what he deserved, and I know I put on a pretty good show when he was killed, but that was more acting than actuality. I was tired of him doing the things he did. Karma has a way of catching up with you, and it was just his time to be caught."

I nodded.

"Something else about me, and this is pretty personal. I don't like my people, especially the men. I hate how they trample over the rest of the world, and they treat us women like we're nothing. Back home in Crimeria, our women rarely have a say in life. We are treated terribly bad by the men, and they don't take care of us the way your people do here in America. My goal is to build something on my own that is so powerful that it gives me a voice that I have never had."

I looked at her for a long time before I could come up with any words. She had so much more going on inside of her than what was on the surface.

"I know a little about you, and I know that you and Tywain make purchases from my Godfather Russell because my father won't mess with you. I understand that if you're out in the world of narcotics, you are trying to seize your portion of the American dream, and I can help you do that. I can plug you into the underworld in a way that you would have never imagined. But in order for that to happen, I would need for you to trust me, for you to pledge your loyalties to me, and respect me as your boss just as you would my father." She flipped her long hair over her shoulders, then cuffed a portion of it behind her ear. "Do you think you would have a problem doing that?"

I shook my head. "When it comes to me and Tywain hustlin', it's always about the best possible plug. If you're sayin' that you can put us in the game the way we're supposed to be put into it, then I'm willin' to do whatever it will take. Pledgin' my loyalty to you will never be a problem."

She smiled, "Well that sounds perfect. There is only one other thing that we need to discuss," she said, licking her red lips.

***

As soon as we made it into her condo, I picked her up by her ass, slamming the door behind me. We crashed into the wall with her back landing against it hard. She bit into my neck so hard, I almost dropped her ass.

"I want you to fuck me, Taurus." She licked my ear lobe, and bit my neck again. "But not the regular way. I want you to rip my clothes off and fuck me like you're raping me. Nothing turns me on more than getting raped by a black man. I want you to punish my pink pussy and take all your anger and frustrations out on it."

She slapped my face so hard that I dropped her ass to the floor. She got up, and walked toward her bedroom. "Come take this cunt."

The stinging on my face, and for some reason, further infuriated me. As she turned around to walk away, I reached and grabbed her by her long blonde hair and pulled her back to me. "White bitch, don't you ever put your hands on me again. You hear me?"

She elbowed me and then slapped my hand away. "Fuck you, what are you going to do?"

I slapped the shit out of her and pushed her to the carpet before straddling her, ripping her Givenchy dress down the middle. I ripped her Burberry bra from her body, exposing her perky tanned titties. I squeezed them, and sucked on the nipples so hard she screamed.

"Ah, fuck yes!"

I tried to pull them off her breast with my lips. At the same time, I ripped her panties off of her with so much force that it raised her off of the floor. It took me a few times before I got them all the way off, but once they were, I trailed my fingers up and down her extremely wet sex lips. "Bitch, open yo legs so I can see if I can fit this black dick in this pussy. You better hope I can't, because if I can, I'm finna rip this muhfucka open!"

She spread her thighs wide. "Please, just fuck the shit out of me. I need it so bad. Fuck me with that black cock!"

I got in between her legs and unbuckled my belt, slipping off my pants, and taking my boxers along with them. My dick was already super hard. I took him by the base and smacked him up against her pussy lips. It made a loud *thunk thunk thunk* sound. She opened her legs wider to the point it looked like she was trying to hit the splits.

"Fuck me right now. I can't take it anymore. I need your dick right now," she begged. She reached down and wrapped her small hand around him, and pulled me to her opening. Right before my head touched her lips, I cocked back and slammed forward, going deeply into her.

She yelped and then moaned, pulling me down by my neck. "Please hurt me, Taurus. Fuck me like you hate my white guts!"

I grabbed her by her neck, and squeezed, taking her right knee and pushing it to her breasts, biting on her neck while I took her so viciously that all she could do was whimper. "Bitch, you want me to kill this shit? You like black dick, huh? Tell me you love it!" I plunged in and out of her at full speed, trying my best to split that li'l pink pussy in two. I could feel her walls squeezing on my tool like a boa constrictor, and honestly, that shit drove me crazy.

"Uh—uh, oh shit, Taurus! I love black dick, baby! It's so big! Fuck this cunt! Kill me with that black dick, Taurus! Ahhhhh!" she screamed, as her body began to tremble and tears started rolling down her cheeks.

I yanked her up by her hair and bent her over the bed, putting my forearm on the small of her back, lining my dick up to her opening, digging her out repeatedly, while she begged me to fuck her until she passed out. Which she did-twice.

Afterwards, we laid in the bed and she told me the entire game plan that she had mapped out for me.

Chapter 3

The next day, I met up with Tywain at one of the trap houses that sold heroin. When I walked into the spot, Tywain was sitting at the table aluminum foiling one gram at a time. He looked exhausted. There were three other young teens around the table foiling up the product as well. All three of them were heavy set with dreadlocks. Though they looked like brothers, they were only cousins.

Martell, the oldest of the three, nodded his head in a *what up* fashion as I sat down at the table. He had a .357 on each hip. Out of the three of them, he was my favorite because he was all about his money. He was quiet, and very direct when he did speak. He was only sixteen years old, and I kind of took him under my wing because I felt we had more in common than the other two. He had lost both of his parents to heroin, and was pretty much an orphan to the streets. I didn't know a lot about him other than he was a hustler.

Deion was the second oldest. He was kind of quiet as well, and had a horrible temper. He kept an Uzi on him at all times and loved to get into drama. He was raised by a dope fiend father that I heard beat him every single day of his life until he killed him. He lived in the streets, and usually slept in whatever trap house we assigned him to. I took a shine to him as well because I liked his heart.

Gary was crazy, too. He talked a lot, and made a lot of jokes, but I had seen him shoot a Spanish dude in the face with a Gauge just because he thought the man was disrespecting his little sister Kesha in his native language. I guess the man thought she was trying to steal out of his store, so he said some pretty strong words to her at first in English, and then switched them over to Spanish. I never found out what was said exactly, but that night, as the man was closing up his store for the night, we were rolling past and Gary asked me to stop the car, which I did. I parked across the street from the store. He ran across it, and encountered the man in the parking lot of the store. No words were said. Gary simply walked up to him, pulled out the gauge, and knocked a hole in the middle of the man's face, before waving me off. I drove away, and he took alleys and gangways all the way back to the trap-house. It was later on that I would find out why he did what he did.

I sat down and started foiling up the product alongside of them. The trap had the A/C going so it felt alright. Usually, it was hot with a bunch of fans blowing out hot ass air, but we had gotten an air conditioner and put it in the downstairs window.

After we finished foiling up a gram, we placed it in the big black garbage bag that was on the side of the table that we sat at. We usually bagged up about three bricks before we opened back up shop.

Tywain made sure that the lil homeys knew what they were doing before we stepped on into the backyard. It had been raining all morning, and at that moment, the sun was just coming out. I pulled out a Garcia Vega that I had stuffed with some tropical loud I'd gotten from Nell. The weed was so fire that it kept you at your highest point for four hours at a time before it started to wear off. I took four deep pulls and passed the blunt to Tywain, who was already sipping lean.

"You never did tell me what that fool Juice said when you went up there to visit him a little while back. Did you know that when they popped him off in the hospital, he had a burner on him?" He took three pulls from the blunt and inhaled it sharply.

"Yeah, my mother told me. But I ain't know at the time." I took the blunt back from him. "Last time I hollered at bro, he was talking about he was gon' body me. No matter how much I tried to explain to that fool the circumstances, the only thing he could wrap his head around was the fact he was locked up."

Tywain shook his head, and then waved his hand through the air. "Fuck him. I'm telling you now, if it comes down to it, I ain't gon' hesitate to body that nigga if he coming gun barking. Ain't no love in these streets, and I already don't like the homey as it is. That nigga so shady."

I nodded my head as I felt the high take over me. I was feeling glorious. "Nastia talking about she wanna plug us in the game."

"Who?" he asked, taking the blunt back from me.

"Nastia, you know, Serge's daughter. She say she got some connects that she gone put us in tune with."

Tywain frowned. "Yo, since when we start fucking wit her on that level? "

"Since everything she said to me made sense. I think that we should at least see what she getting at. I mean, we really ain't got nothing to lose. If she thinking that she owes me her life, then who am I to change her feelings. I think the smartest thing for us to do is see where she going wit shit. If she ain't on nothing, then we keep it moving. It's as simple as that."

Tywain gave me a knowing look. "You fucked that bitch, didn't you?"

I couldn't help but laugh out loud. "What?"

"Nigga, you heard me. You fucked that bitch and now she trying to give you the world." He shook his head. "You somethin' else. Every time you put yo dick in one of these hoes, the next thing you know, they acting super psychotic." He sipped his Lean.

"Bro, it ain't even about that. I think shorty just wanna be her own boss or something. She got a few connects that she wanna capitalize off of, and she wanna use us to make that happen."

"You sure it's us, and not just you? "

"One hundred percent. We must've sat up talking about everything for three hours straight. So she know what it is. All I'm waiting for now is for her to reach out to me, and we'll see what comes next."

***

She reached out to me two weeks later. Me and Tywain met up with her at the airport. She met us with hugs, and then we followed her until we wound up at a ducked off hangar that had an all-white small airplane inside. There were two body guards that stood heavily armed on each side of the plane's door entrance. We followed her past this point and onto the plane.

The plane was decked out with flat screen TVs everywhere. The passenger's seats were all pink leather, and in front of each one was a bottle of Champagne sitting on ice inside of a rose gold bow. There were two flight attendants that looked as if they were mixed with black and something exotic because their skin was the color of mine, but they had long curly hair, and Spanish features.

The plane also had a mini refrigerator by each chair. I couldn't see what was inside of them, but I assumed it had to be some sort of food, or drinks. Nastia pointed to the seats and told us to make ourselves comfortable. She turned to Tywain.

"These are my girls. Anything you want from them, they will give to you with no questions asked."

"What about me?" I asked, feeling a little jealous. Those chicks were bad as hell. I had a few things I wanted to ask of them. She must've saw the lust in my eyes as I looked them up and down.

"You don't even think about it. If you want anything taken care of, I'll be the one doing that for you. Besides, we need to talk so I can prepare you for what's to come."

I saw the big beefy guards get on to the plane and slam the door. Then I followed Nastia into a subsection of the plane that had a door on it. It led to a small bedroom. We stepped into it and closed the door. It blew my mind when I heard Trey Songz bellowing out of the speakers. I couldn't help but to laugh a little bit.

She sat on the edge of the bed. I sat beside her, and kissed her neck. She moaned, grabbed a remote control, and a flat screen television dropped from the ceiling. "These are the men that we will be meeting in about three hours. She stood up and pointed to the screen. "His name is Hood Rich. He is one of the most influential business men in the narcotics underworld. He has the best product that has ever come under the heroin umbrella. He calls his product The Rebirth. It is a chemically enhanced heroin that allows users to feel as if they are getting high for the first time, every single time they use the product. The drug is so strong that the users become physically dependent upon it so badly that it's all they want to do all day long. It becomes the center of their lives. Hood Rich is the co-creator of the said drug."

I looked over at the brown skinned man with the light colored eyes, and I could have sworn I was familiar with him. He looked very young, but at the same time older, as if he had taken good care of himself. The picture of him on the screen showed him standing on the side of an all red Porsche.

She pointed to the next man. "His name is Meech. He is Hood Rich's right hand man, and co-creator of The Rebirth. They have been running pals since they were children. Anything Hood Rich does, Meech knows about it, and vice versa. Both men are filthy rich, and they head the narcotics underworld."

She pushed something on the remote control that allowed for the screen to change to another frozen shot. I noted they were pictures of project buildings. "Hood Rich and Meech became rich the day they took over these project buildings known as the Robert Taylor Homes. Legend has it that they bum rushed the apartments inside and forced every adult to inject The Rebirth. After this sting, they took over the State Way projects the same way, and before you knew it, they had nearly the entire city hooked on The Rebirth."

"So all of these dudes operate out of Chicago?" I asked, now starting to remember why Hood Rich seemed so familiar to me.

She nodded. "That is where they began, and are now all over the United Kingdom, and a few other countries. Because of their Rebirth, they have managed to take the world by storm. They have caused an epidemic. Heroin is taking the world by storm. But not just any heroin, their version of heroin."

I was confused. "So why are you telling me all of this?"

"Because its best that you know who you're meeting with and not go in front of them with blind eyes to their past. These are business men that are trying to break into Russia, and my father is the only man standing in their way. I am their key. If they do right by me, I'll do whatever it takes to make my father happy." She smiled wickedly. "He loves his little girl in more ways than one."

I could hear moaning in the next room and I figured Tywain must not have waited long before he was fucking the two dames. I couldn't help but to laugh at that. The homey never played games about going for what he wanted.

Nastia rubbed my chest. "I am going to get my hands on The Rebirth, and I want you to infect the south, starting with Memphis. It's the only part of the States that they have not touched because my father has prevented them from cornering the market in honor of Russell. Well, to hell with that. I never liked Russell anyway. Besides, he's gotten rich enough off my family's pull. It's time a real sheriff came into town, and he goes by the name of my favorite zodiac sign." She pushed me to the bed and straddled me, laying her head on my chest. "I just want to make you so happy, Taurus. I want you to be bigger than all of the rest of those sharks in the water. I want you to own me, and I want to own you just as much. You're so perfect for me." She kissed my chest, put her hand under my Polo shirt, and rubbed my abs.

By the time the plane landed, Nastia and I were both just waking up. Yawning, she climbed out of the bed when somebody knocked on the door. "Who is it?" she asked, stretching her arms over her head.

One of the bodyguards was standing in the doorway explaining to her that we had reached our destination. We stepped right off of the plane and loaded up into an all-black on black Helicopter. Tywain and I sat in the back with our head gear on. All I could do was shake my head because the reality was that we had stepped off one luxurious thing and boarded the next. That was living, and how I preferred to travel.

About an hour later, the chopper landed on top of the John Hancock building in Chicago. We were escorted by the bodyguards onto the roof of the building, and through a small door that took us to an elevator. We took the elevator downward until it reached the designated floor. The doors opened to reveal a board room where Hood Rich and Meech were sitting at the table with ten heavily armed bodyguards surrounding them.

As soon as Hood Rich saw Nastia, he walked up to her and wrapped her in his arms, kissing her on both cheeks. "How have you been, Princess?"

She bowed her head. "I'm quite alright. As you can see, I've brought some people with me that I would love for you to meet." She turned around and fanned her hand toward me and Tywain.

Meech was the next to wrap her in his arms. I saw his hands go a little lower until they were resting on her small booty, and then he squeezed her cheeks. She pulled his hands away from her, and turned around to look at me, her face bright red. "Meech, I've told you about that already."

He frowned. "Since when?"

She waved him off. "Anyway, this is Taurus, the young man I've been telling you about. And this is his right-hand man, Tywain. They are your gateways into Russia. You take care of them, and I'll give you the key to the Communist World."

They looked me over for a long time before they invited us to sit down. Tywain sat by me with a look on his face that said he didn't care who they were. I could tell that he didn't like how they were acting towards us. They barely paid us any mind at all. They gave most of their attention to Nastia.

Finally, Hood Rich quieted down the board room and took his place at the head of the table. "We have been forbidden to enter into the south with our extremely potent product, and now we're given the green light to seal up those territories down low, but only if we work through you two. Now ain't that a bitch?" he said, looking around the room. "However, the southern states aren't what's important to us. He stood up, we want Russia, and if the only way we get access into Russia is through the two of you, then let's make this happen."

Meech stood and pulled down a projector screen. The lights were turned off as he began his presentation. When the film started, it showed the buildings of Orange Mound. "This is where we will have you implant The Rebirth. This is the heart and soul of Memphis. Well, this place and this one."

Black Haven's buildings appeared on the screen. "If you infect these two areas with our drug, you will be able to build up your Dynasty. These are the two biggest drug infested areas in all of Memphis. If you monopolize the market in these two areas, you will run the game."

Hood Rich stood back up. "We are willing to sell you kilos of The Rebirth for ten thousand dollars apiece. But keep in mind that the average kilo of The Rebirth was no less than fifty. Take this as a show of our appreciation."

Meech took over, "Not only will we sell you the kilos for ten thousand dollars apiece, but the work you'll get will be fresh and pure. I will whip it myself, every batch, every single time." He straightened his tie that coordinated with his Tom Ford business suit. "Now The Rebirth is an extremely potent drug. Your customers will give you their lives for it. However, if they are denied the right to have it, they will take your life with no hesitation. You must put a system in place where you are able to have all forms of their money, but they will also never be without the drug. For that purpose, we have drafted you a blue print on how to market The Rebirth most successfully. Just a couple pages out of our book, if you will." He laughed and looked at Meech.

Meech gave him a stern face, before looking to me. "This is not a game. These are real lives that you will be taking over, so everything you do must be with strategy. Take nothing for granted and trust no one. The Rebirth brings out the ugly in everybody."

We stayed in that meeting with them lacing us for three hours. I made sure that I mentally soaked up every piece of game they threw at us. They were the professionals, and we were to be using their product. I felt it imperative to hang on to their every word.

Chapter 4

I found out Juice had got stabbed eleven times in prison, after the Hood Rich and Meech business meeting. Me and Shakia was coming from one of the doctor's appointments when she told me that she had a craving for a Gyro with cheese and mustard. I didn't know what the baby was thinking inside of her stomach to have had a taste for something like that, but I was on my way to Jahrome's Gyros, when Princess pulled behind my truck, and started honking her horn like crazy.

She pulled up to my driver's windows and rolled her passenger's window down. Snow was falling lightly, and it was very windy. We were at a stop light right before getting to Jahrome's Gyros. The restaurant was no more than a half a block away. I hollered out of the window for her to follow me into parking lot. She nodded that she would.

After she got there, I gave Shakia a blue face hundred-dollar bill and told her to get whatever she wanted. As soon as she got out of the car, Princess slid into the passenger's seat.

"Juice got stabbed up last night. They hit him eleven times, all in his back. I don't know if he's okay or what because when I called the prison, they wouldn't give me any more details." She looked stressed out and like she'd lost some weight, and she was already a very small female.

"Do you know who did it?" I asked, grabbing her hand and trying to rub it before she snatched it away from me.

"Don't touch me right now. I'm upset, because none of this would have happened if you hadn't allowed that chick to set him up. Now he could be dead." I saw a tear sail down her cheek. "And no, I don't know who did it but I'm pretty sure he does."

I really didn't feel no type of way about that nigga, Juice, getting hit up. I knew bro was shiesty and he had fucked over a lot of niggas. Sooner or later things had to catch up to him. I felt bad for Princess because she seemed traumatized! It seemed like she was genuinely concerned for his well being and a part of me felt disgusted because Juice was a low life, who had crazy enemies all over the system, so it wasn't no telling who had hit him up and why. "Princess, is there anything that I can do for you?"

She lowered her head. "I miss my brother. We still don't know where he is. But Juice say he got some of his homies out looking for him, so hopefully they'll find him soon. Other than that, I'm flat broke. I don't have a red cent to my name, so if you could hit my hand with a few bucks, that'll be cool. I'll probably wind up putting half of it on Juice's books anyway. I need to make sure he's straight in there."

I thought it was real fucked up that she was trying to do so much for my brother when he was the one that killed hers in cold blood. Juice was cold-hearted. There was no way I could carry on with a charade like that. That was so foul to me.

As she finished talking, Shakia came back to the truck and stood by the passenger's door, looking at Princess like she was crazy. Princess saw her standing there and rolled her eyes. Then she opened the back door of the truck for her. Shakia paused for a few moments holding the bag of food staring Princess down, but then she gave in and climbed into the back, slamming the door so hard the whole truck rocked.

I went into my pocket and pulled out a knot of hundreds. I counted off fifty of them and gave them to Princess. "Here you go, this should hold you for a couple days, and don't worry about sending none of it to Juice because I'm gon' send him a few bands through Money Gram. You take that paper and get yourself together. I'll link up with you later on tonight or something."

She smiled weakly. "Thank you, bro. I know you and your brother at odds, but I don't wanna be in the middle of that. You and I have always been straight so I wanna keep it that way." She leaned forward and hugged me tightly, before kissing me on the cheek. "You know I'mma pay you back for this."

I kissed her forehead. "No you ain't. Later on we gon' get together so I can make sure you straight. I don't want you thinking that you out here alone, because you not."

Shakia cleared her throat loudly in the backseat. "Taurus, it's time for us to get going. I can feel the baby gettin' irritated," she said, rubbing her stomach.

Princess gave me a knowing look. "Well, thanks again, Taurus, and I will see you tonight, right?"

I nodded. "Fa sho', I gotta make sure you straight before my head hit that pillow."

She smiled, and I could see a little light come into her eyes. She turned to the back seat. "Oh, and congratulations, Shakia. I don't think I ever told you that. I heard you're having a little girl. That's what's up."

Shakia curled her lip. "I ain't havin' a girl, *we* are havin' a girl. We, meanin' me and Taurus. So, I think you should congratulate him, too."

Princess shook her head, and laughed. "Anyway, y'all take care and be safe out here." She got out of the truck and left the door open for Shakia.

As soon as Shakia got back into the front of the truck, she slammed the door so hard, I was afraid she might have broken the window. "I can't stand that skinny bitch," she said, wrapping her arms around herself.

I was so irritated with her that I wanted to snap, but I kept my composure. It seemed like every time we got together, she always found something to be mad about. That tune was getting old.

"And then you ain't say nothing to this bitch when she disrespected our child."

I pulled the truck out of the parking lot, nearly hitting some dude that rolled up out of nowhere on a Moped. He whipped his bike on to the sidewalk and kept on going like nothing ever happened. "When did she disrespect our child?"

She exhaled loudly. "She disrespected her when she made it seem like she didn't belong to you, that's when." She rolled her eyes, and looked back out of her window. "Then, why you give her so much money? That bitch don't need all that. You act like she your woman or something. You don't even give me that kind of money no more."

"Is that why you really mad? Are you mad because I'm lookin' out for her and you jealous? If so, get over it, because you ain't running shit. I told you that already. All you gotta do is stay in yo place, and navigate in the lane I'm giving you. Every time you step outside of that, we wind up falling off, and then I don't see you until the next doctor's appointment. I can't see how you don't get that." I stepped on the gas because I was ready to drop her ass off.

We rode in silence for about ten minutes. Then, when I got about five minutes away from her house, she started crying. "I'm sorry, Taurus. I just don't like when other females be under you like that. Then, she all needy for you, and making sure you gone get up with her tonight. That kills me to hear because I would like to be under you all night. But when was the last time that happened?" She closed her eyes and cried harder. "All I wanna do is give you a healthy baby so you will love me like nobody else do."

As I drove away from dropping her off, everything that she'd said ran through my mind. Sometimes I wondered if I was doing her wrong because I didn't settle down and be with her. I did have a lot of love for her, but I guess somewhere along the way my respect for her had died out. She mostly irritated me more than anything. At one point, I had found her extremely gorgeous, but ever since I caught her and my brother in the act, I didn't feel any urges towards her whatsoever.

Princess had snatched up a small apartment on Chambers Street. That was on the west side of town, and mostly Asians stayed out in that area. When I pulled up in front of her building, she was just pulling up with a car full of groceries.

I took most of the bags in for her, and then helped her put everything away while she tried to get me talking.

"I don't understand what you see in her?" she said as she stood on her tippy toes to put the raviolis into the cabinet. She was so short. I found that to be crazily hot. I was trying my best to not let it get to me. She had on some tight ass capris that hugged her ass perfectly. Every time she tried to reach further into the cabinet to put more can goods away, the pants would go into her ass crack.

"See in who?" I asked, knowing damn well who she was talking about. I just wanted to keep her talking so I could check out her lil body.

"Shakia. I don't see how you started messing with her in the first place. I mean, she ain't even all that, especially not to be giving her a child. That mean you gotta be with her for the rest of your life. Now that gotta suck."

I was hearing what she was saying, but it wasn't really registering because I was visually lusting. I know most people would probably think that I was bogus for lusting over my brother's girl or whatever. But trust me, that nigga Juice didn't care about her like that, at least from what I could tell. I figured Princess was just convenient.

"Well do it?"

"Do what?" I asked, watching her bend over, and seeing her pink thong expose itself at the top of her low rise jeans.

"Do it suck having to be with her for the rest of your life, knowing that you'll never be happy with her?" She stood up and put her hand on her hip, looking me in the eye, almost challenging me.

I shrugged my shoulders. "Ain't nothing in stone yet. Once I get a paternity test, then we'll see about all that forever shit you screaming. If it's my daughter, then I got my baby for life. If not, I'm make sure Shakia straight from a distance, but I can't be with her like that. We just don't click."

Princess walked up to me and stood in my face. "Oh yeah, and who do you click with?" She licked her lips, and sucked on her bottom one, leaving it wet and shiny.

I looked down on her and I could feel my heartbeats speed up. She took another step forward and I felt myself becoming hard. My dick went straight upward and started to peek out of my waistband. I could feel it throbbing against my stomach.

"Well?"

I snatched her little ass up so fast that I didn't even know I was doing it. All I heard was her yelp, and then she was up against the wall with her legs wrapped around me, and us tonguing each other like we were in a porno movie. I mean, she sucked on my lips, and moaned into my ear while I held her ass in the palms of my hands. I squeezed that perfect ass, and trailed my fingers into her crease, where there was so much heat that it was like she was hiding a furnace between her legs.

She licked my neck, and bit me so hard that I groaned out in pain. But I loved the feel of it. I felt her trying to take my wife beater off by pulling it over my head, and I allowed that to happen. I still had her squished against the wall. I was naked from the waist up with her squeezing my stomach muscles.

"I been wantin' to get my hands on this stomach since the first day I met you." She scratched me a little, before running the palms of her hands over the abs.

I fell to the floor with her, ripping off her tank top and the matching pink bra. Her breasts were small, about the size of A-cups, but the nipples were huge. They were nice and round, almost covering the entire globe, and they looked like dark brown pacifiers. I tried to fit one whole tittie into my mouth, and was successful. At the same time, I twirled my tongue around the big nipple, before pulling on it with my lip and teeth.

She moaned and opened her legs wide. I saw her hands unbuttoning her jeans, and then she snuck one of them inside, where she got to playing with her own pussy. It was one of the hottest things I had ever seen in my life.

"Damn, this shit feel good, Taurus. Just let me keep rubbin' your stomach while I get off." The harder she squeezed my abs, the faster her fingers moved inside of her panties. Her jerking movements started to drive me crazy. I felt like I was getting light headed. I had never seen a woman get herself off before and it was doing something to me.

When she screamed that she was coming, and started humping her fingers, I snapped. I pulled her jeans all the way off and exposed the fact that she had three fingers deep inside of her pussy. I pulled them out of her and sucked them clean. Then I flipped her on to her stomach, and got to sucking all over that ass. I put hickeys all up and down her ass cheeks, before taking my tongue and slurping up her juices. I held that ass wide open and licked up every drop while she diddled her clitoris under me until she came again.

She had me lay on my back. "Okay, Taurus, look, as bad as I wanna give you this pussy, I can't because I don't wanna do your brother like that. But peep this." She laid on top of me and opened her pussy lips, grabbing my dick and squeezing it. "Damn, you got a big ass dick. I didn't expect all of this." She took my dick head and put it between her pussy lips. Then she got to grinding on me so good that I didn't even care if I was able to go into the pussy. Her shit was so wet, and so fat that I was content with what she was doing, especially when she got to talkin' that shit to me.

"You know you ain't right. You got me rubbing my pussy all over this big dick. I'm supposed to be yo brother's girl, and you got my pussy wide open. Uh, oh shit," she moaned as I pinched her nipples.

Because she was so short, her scalp was all under my nose and it was like her pheromones were going up my nose. I got to feeling all kinds of crazy. I grabbed her ass and made her grind into me harder. More than once, my dick head went into her and she pulled it out.

"Yes, yes, yes, Taurus, awh shit, yes," she moaned, sucking on my neck. I grabbed her, and smashed her down into me, and then came all over her lips, just as she screamed and came. She got onto her knees and licked up our combined juices hungrily while I ran my fingers through her hair.

Afterward, we laid right there on the carpet while she rubbed my abs. "I know I'm bogus as hell for doing that, but I can't lie, I been thinking about you like crazy. I mean, it ain't like me and Juice married or nothing." She raised her head to look into my face. "Why are you so quiet? Are you having regrets now or something?"

"You want me to be honest with you?" I asked, trailing my hand down and cupping her pussy. I spread the lips with my fingers, and slid my middle one in her.

She moaned and raised her hips into the air, swallowing my whole finger. Her cave felt hot, and like velvet. "Yes, bro, go ahead and be honest." She closed her eyes as my finger worked in and out of her.

"I'm just trying to figure out why you ain't let me murder this pussy fa real." I kissed her on the neck, and sucked it. "I mean, we already went far enough."

She pumped my dick and squeezed it tightly. "This is a big ass dick, Taurus. That nigga Juice a try to go in after he get out, feel what you done, and know I been fucking around. I can't have that drama like that. Plus, I feel like it's okay to play around with you, just as long as we don't go all the way. "

I gave her a look that said she was out of her mind. "Yeah, well, I want you to make me come one more time, and then we can get up. How do that sound?"

She smiled, took my dick, and rubbed it all over her face before sliding it all the way to the back of her throat. She popped it out. "After I finish, you gotta do me."

All I could muster was, "Bet."

That night, I left, and came back dropping her off six pounds of Tropical Loud. "Everything you make from this is supposed to go toward your rent, bills, and hitting Juice books. Let me know when you run out and I'mma hit you again. Here go five more gees to make sure you all the way straight. Hit me whenever.

Chapter 5

"I'm giving you two kilos of this Meth shit, and I want you to do your thing over here. You always talking about your cousins be crowding your space, so I'mma give you your own shit. I expect you to make it happen," Tywain said, dropping the bricks on the table before Martell.

"What about them Asian Bloodz that be looking at me all crazy every time we roll up to this building? I told you I knocked one of them out at school after the nigga ran up on me asking me about one of they hoes I was supposed to have gotten pregnant. "

I wrapped my arm around him. "Don't worry about them. We got all that shit handled. All you gotta do is stay in here and get money. We gone let you build up your own crew, too. But keep in mind that whoever you bring into this shit, you're responsible for. So choose wisely."

Tywain came around the table and stood in front of him. He placed his hands on both of Martell's shoulders. "Yo, you know I love you, right?"

Martell nodded. "Yea, I know that, big homey, without a shadow of a doubt."

Tywain took the .44 Desert Eagle out of the small of his back and put it to Martell's forehead. "We're giving you a position of power. That means that anything you do reflects back on us one way or the other. If you make any mistakes, there will be no second chances. Do you understand that?"

Martell curled his upper lip. He leaned his head further into the gun. "If I make a mistake, I don't need a second chance. Kill me and bury me a muthafuckin' G!"

Tywain nodded. "That's what the fuck I'm talking about. That's why we putting you in charge of this Meth shit. It's because you got that killa instinct. You gone make this shit your own. Keep our business fresh. I need for you to keep fucking with the Asian homey and keep the product potent. We'll give you thirty percent of every kilo, and a bonus five gees every Friday. This your operation, we'll just be your overseers. However you want this business to run, it's on you. "

Martell nodded with tears running down his cheeks. "Ain't no muhfucka ever gave me a chance. Y'all the only ones that cared enough to believe in me. I'll die for you niggas, man, that's my word." He hugged us, and I patted his back.

That same day, we set Deion up over on Buffum. It was a large apartment complex that was run by the East Indians that had just moved to Memphis. There was an older Indian by the name of Jock that held the most pull for their community. We had to hit him off with ten gees every other week just to receive the go ahead to operate on Indian turf.

We put five bricks of cocaine in Deion's lap, all powder and barely touched. He had a few of his lil homies that ran under him that pledged their loyalties. They were a small crew of head busters. Crazy, but all about their paper. Before the Indians moved in, Deion had grown up in that complex, so he knew the area very well. One of the officers that worked that beat used to mess with his aunty, so it wasn't that hard to get him and his partner on the pay roll. Two thousand dollars a week, and that was two thousand one week for one and another two thousand for the other the following week.

Deion pledged his loyalties in blood to me and Tywain, and we made a vow that as long as he handled his business, we'd keep him rich. Tywain put the Desert Eagle to his head, just like he'd done Martell, and Deion didn't flinch. I could tell that lil homey was serious about his, and so was his lil crew. They all had dreadlocks, and called themselves the Comma Kids.

In exchange for his hustle, Deion would get thirty percent off of each kilo, and five gees every week.

Since Gary had grown up within a heroin addicted family, we decided to put him in charge of what he knew best. I'd watched the kid whip heroin like it was mashed potatoes way before we got in tune with Hood Rich and Meech's Rebirth. We felt that if we dropped that into his lap with all that potency, he would make a miracle happen, and that was something that we needed. He was a go getter anyway. We felt that all we needed to do was to put a little faith in him.

We hadn't received our first shipment of The Rebirth just yet, but the heroin we had was real nice. We decided to drop five kilos of that into his lap. Once again Tywain put the *ratchet* to another one of their foreheads, and he didn't crumble either. He was less emotional about the whole ordeal, but what I saw in him was a souljah.

"Remember, you are to get your troops ready because we gone be taking over this whole complex by force. We want everybody in this muhfucka shooting our dope. That's the only way we gon' reach them proper commas."

"You already know, all you gotta do is say the word and I'mma make it happen for the family. We Comma Kids over here, too. My cousins ain't the only ones that's gone make y'all proud, trust and believe that."

After we got the lil homeys squared away, me and Tywain sat down with a dude name Pooky. Pooky was one of those heroin addicts that used to be a kingpin but started using their own supply and fell all the way off. He was born and raised in Orange Mound and could tell you everybody that lived there, and who their family was all over Memphis. We decided to add him to the payroll because he could give us the real blueprints of the Mound.

Although we had not been sent our shipment of The Rebirth, we did have a kilo to dibble and dab with. I took out about a gram and poured it on to the small plate in front of Pooky. He rolled up his sleeves, and started to tie a belt around his arm.

"If this shit is as good as you say it is, you gone be a rich nigga, I can tell you that now."

I whipped the work for him, and got it ready for him to inject. I could see that he was pulling the belt real tight, so much so that a thick vein popped up in his left forearm.

I put my latex gloves on and rubbed it for a second. "That's where you want this shit?"

He nodded. "Yeah, mane, you hit me in that bitch right there and I'm gone party."

I stuck the tip of the needle in and injected him, pushing the feeder all the way to the bottom until all of the drugs were gone. He sat in his chair for a brief second, and then his eyes got really bucked, and his head fell to his chest. Then he took his shirt off, followed by his pants. He kicked them off as if they were on fire.

"This that shit here, mane. Look, blood, I'm tellin' you, this that shit!" He took his boxers off and sat there ass naked in the chair with his hand wrapped around his dick. I threw his shirt over his lap. "Fuck all that, tell me how it's making you feel."

He nodded out in the chair in one moment, the next, he popped his head up. "Check this out, mane, this shit y'all got rockin' got me feelin' like I'm gettin' fucked by Beyoncé. At the same time, she shootin' me up with the best uncut dope in the world. Y'all ain't stepped on this shit. I can tell. Got me feelin' like my first high."

His broad came into the room with a nappy small afro. Her white sundress was covered in Kool-Aid stains. Tywain sat her down and pumped her up with The Rebirth. Before he took the needle out of her arm, she already had her legs wide open and her tongue sticking out of her mouth.

"That's the shit right there, play boy." She nodded out on the couch and drool came out of the corners of her mouth.

Me and Tywain waited about an hour before we smiled at each other, silently celebrating the fact that they were still high and in a deep foggy daze. Before we left we had Pooky give us the entire run down of the complex. It looked like it wasn't going to be an easy task of bum rushing, or doing shit the way Hood Rich and Meech had said they did things. In order to pull off their moves, we would've had to cause a lot of bloodshed, so we decided to go a different route.

We received our first shipment of The Rebirth that weekend. Nastia had a friend's husband that worked at Fed Ex. She had him deliver the product to us at the old recycling plant outside of Burleigh. When the big truck pulled in, me and Tywain were seated in his Lexus truck with Nastia in the back massaging my shoulders.

"I'm tellin' you guys that when this product hits Memphis, you'll be filthy rich. It shouldn't take us no time to venture out into Georgia, Florida, and Alabama. The sky is the limit. I'm so fuckin' excited I can't contain myself. Aren't you, baby?" she asked, rubbing my chest while she leaned over the back of my seat.

"Yeah, I just want us to get it in our hands, and then we'll be happy."

Tywain nodded, "That's right. Ain't shit to celebrate about until we get the shipment and bounce wit it."

That was when the Fed Ex truck rolled into the old Recycling plant and parked on the side of our truck. We got out, heavily armed, me holding a M90, and Tywain had an AK-47 in his hands.

Martell, Deion, and Gary were also in place, heavily armed and already given the order to chop anything that looked funny.

And if it was a set up, they were told to kill every cop in sight. But we ain't have to exercise none of those orders. When the white man opened the back of the truck, we saw a big cardboard box. It was the only box left in the truck. I climbed into the truck and slit the box open on the side, and a teddy bear fell out. It was a big one, and heavier than what I was accustomed to.

"Be careful with that, Taurus. The product is inside of those teddies. The teddy bears are hollowed out with aluminum foil, and The Rebirth has been poured into them. Each teddy bear has nine ounces of The Rebirth inside of it. We should have a total of two hundred teddy bears. Nine times two hundred is eighteen hundred ounces. That's fifty kilos of pure uncut Rebirth."

I took my Swiss Army knife and cut into the bear. A little of the powder spilled, about an eighth of a gram. "Lets go. Everything good."

We packed up the bears into the mini van that Gary drove, and took them back to our trap over on Locust Street. We must've stayed up for the next fourteen hours, sifting and packaging The Rebirth. I couldn't wipe the big smile off of my face.

The next morning, I woke up Tywain and told him that I was going to see my pops because he had sent word to me through my mother. I told the homey that I would be back later that afternoon.

When I finally got inside of my pop's prison, after all of the metal detector drama, and being frisked like I was the one in prison, I had time to collect my thoughts while I got about fifty dollars' worth of dollar coins for us to eat with.

As I sat there in my gray chair waiting for him to come out, I had so many thoughts running through my mind. It had almost been a year since I'd seen my old man. I didn't really know what to say to him. I was trying to put together an opening in my head when he came through the door looking like a short version of George Foreman. I stood up.

He walked right up to me and wrapped his massive arms around me. "Baby boy, it feels good to see you."

I hugged him tightly and patted his back. "It feel good to see you, too, pops."

I had all kinds of burgers and cheese pizzas all over the table. Anything that was in the machine that didn't have pork in it was on our table, damn near. I saw him looking down at everything and I laughed. "I didn't know what you would want so I just got a little bit of everything."

He had a long bushy beard. He looked just like one of those Muslims from overseas. "Yeah, that's gratitude, sun. I appreciate it. These crackers got me in here starvin'. If you ain't hit my books the way you do, I'd be about a hundred pounds."

"You know I got you," I said, looking around the crowded room. It was baby momma central. I saw all kinds of females with kids walking around that joker. Some of them were thick as hell, too.

"So what's up wit you and Juice? Is what he telling me the truth?" he asked, reaching and opening up a Sprite.

"Nall, pop, it ain't nothing like that. That fool was out here reckless. The stuff he was doing was puttin' my mother and sister at risk. We have to protect the only two females in our family. He wasn't doing that."

He took the cheese pizza out of the wrapper and took a big bite from it. "How do you mean?"

"He messed around with the wrong people that were so connected that it wouldn't have taken nothing for them to wipe all of us out, including you in here. "

He chewed with his mouth closed, and one nostril flared. "You talking about Serge, the Russian. Am I right?"

I felt chills go down my spine. "How did you know that?"

"It's not just that. Son, I am the one that told your brother to snatch that bitch and her brother up. Your brother was just following my orders." He wiped his mouth on a napkin. "You see, I knew that Juice would make the mistake of bringing that dope fiend Pac Man along for the trip, and I knew that Pac Man would piss him off so bad that he would kill him. Your brother has a temper just like me, but none of my smarts. You have all of my smarts and just the right amount of my temper. You are the smartest seed of my loins." He took another bite of the pizza, and washed it down with more of the Sprite.

"Pops, you blowing my mind right now. So what are you saying exactly?" I leaned in closer to him, looking into his menacing eyes.

"I knew that if Juice called you after Pac Man screwed everything up, you would fix it. I gave the order for your brother to kill Pac Man. I knew that Nastia would fall for you because she is in love with black dick. Her mother is the same way. Juice needed to play the role of an angry bandit, and you of the hero. When he killed Pac Man in front of her, that led her to believe that she would eventually be next, when all along, she is too valuable of a chess piece. I needed for you to rescue her. You rescue her and she will catapult our family into the big leagues after she falls in love with you. *Now*, tell me about your meeting with Hood Rich?"

I damn near jumped out of my seat. Now shit was really starting to get real. I was about to ask him how he knew about that, but I decided against it.

"Our meeting was a success. We got our first shipments of The Rebirth last night, and we gone look to make it happen with it within the next couple of days, as soon as we figure out how to get it into the systems of everybody in town."

He shook his head. "I don't want you using the playbook that they used back in Chicago. They made a whole lot of enemies like that. And for the rest of their lives, they will be looking over their shoulders, which is why they are trying to venture out into Russia. This family has to take a more sensible, strategic approach. We are building a Dynasty through you, son. You have always been my chosen one."

"I couldn't tell because you never cuffed me. You always made sure that Juice was learning at your heels, but you kept me at arm's length. I never understood that." I flared my nostrils as I recalled some of those moments when I wanted to be with them and he denied me that right.

"I did exactly what I was supposed to do. I kept Juice close because I had to worry about him. With you, I never worried because you had the abilities to see things in your mind, and make them operate in a manner that Juice did not." He took a sip of the Sprite, swishing it around his mouth. "You know, I always thought that you would kill Juice first, and Gotto last. That is the only place you caught me off guard. I guess your brother had it coming." He shrugged his shoulders. "I don't care. He was soft, ashes to ashes, dust to dust." He leaned into my face. "Hood Rich is our family's in into the underworld. He is plugged with the head of the five Mafia families, the great Don Ciarpaglini. Now that we are in business with him, it allows for our family to elevate into the next level. You are the key, son. Our Dynasty starts with you. Trust me when I tell you that I am doing my part from right here. I am clocking and logging your every move. Be careful because it is already predestined that either you are going to kill Juice, or Juice is going to kill you."

I felt a cold shudder go down my back. My father had been telling me that ever since I was fourteen years old. I didn't want to kill my oldest brother, but I wouldn't hesitate to pull the trigger if he tried to kill me either. My heart was turning colder, yet I still found it hard to lose my common sense. My father put a lot on my brain. I didn't know how he knew half the shit he knew, but then again, he was my old man. He had survived in the game a long time. I was his seed. He knew me, as much as I hated to admit that. I got to wondering if I was playing my own version of the game, or if I was nothing more than a controller to my pops' PlayStation.

Chapter 6

My mother had decided to move herself and my sister out to Jackson, Mississippi where my Aunty Vanessa stayed. Vanessa was her youngest sister. She was twenty-three years old, and looked just like my mother, with the exception of her eyes that were hazel.

Vanessa was a country girl at heart, and one of the sweetest people I had ever met. Since I was preparing to jump head first into the game, I thought I would go and spend some time with my mother and sister because I had not physically seen them in nearly six months at that time.

Nastia bought me a black and red Mercedes truck. It was a 2017, all custom interior. I got the black and red leather Louis Vuitton seats, and the floor mats to match. I was on a Louis kick at that time, and everything I wore or drove had to fit into that scheme of things.

I surprised my mother by pulling up on her and my sister as they were coming from church. Now the whole time my mother had been with my father, she acted as if she practiced Islam around him. But I would often hear her praying the Lord's Prayer. I even did it with her at times. I personally leaned more toward Jehovah because when I was little, my mother used to tell me about him when I got scared of there being a monster under my bed.

My father tended to try and scare Allah into us, whereas my mother spoke lovingly about Jehovah, and Jesus Christ. So when I prayed, I sent my prayers up to Jehovah, although quiet as it's kept, I felt like Jehovah and Allah were the same God.

My sister was the first to see me. She was holding an arm full of Roses, and when she saw me, she dropped them to the ground and screamed, running full speed until she got into the street and jumped into my arms.

"Taurus, oh my god, I'm so happy to see you!" She wrapped her legs around me and hugged me tight.

"I'm happy to see you, too, princess. How have you been?"

It must have taken my mother's brain a little while to compute that I was actually there because, as I held my sister in my arms, I saw her face go through an array of changes. At first she looked unaffected, and then she blinked three times, followed by her eyes bugging out of her head. The next thing I knew, she screamed and ran toward me at full speed, after dropping her church fan.

I barely put my sister down before she jumped into my arms and kissed me on the lips with so much force that I almost dropped her. I had to hoist her up, and hold on to her more tightly.

When I put her down, she took a step back, and then wrapped her arms around my neck. "I missed you so much, baby." She smacked me on the arm. "What took you so long to come out here?"

"Yeah, we ain't seen you in forever. You've missed my birthday and everything," Mary said, lowering her head.

I put my arm around both of them and we walked back toward the church. "I had a lot of business to take care of back home. If I could have gotten here one day sooner, I would have." I kissed both of them on the cheek. "I missed y'all like crazy, too."

A high yellow female with one of the coldest figures I had ever seen came down the church steps and hugged my mother. I was so busy looking at her body that I didn't even get the chance to make out her face before she was hugging her. But when she took a step back and screamed, I damn near jumped out of my skin.

"I know that ain't my nephew looking all muscle bound and stuff. Boy! You better get over here and give me a hug," Vanessa said, holding her arms wide open.

As soon as I saw that it was her, I got to feeling a little guilty for peeping her the way that I did. I wrapped her into my arms and kissed her on the cheek, and she did the same to me. I noted that she smelled really good, too.

"How have you been?" I asked, wrapping my arm back around my mother and sister.

She rubbed my chest with her hand, and then fanned herself with the paper makeshift fan that they always handed out in their church. "Honey, I'm blessed by the best. I can't complain. Right now I'm in the mist of opening up my own restaurant down here so I can give all of these folk a taste of Southern Love, and that's just what I'm gone name my restaurant, too." She closed her eyes and smiled like she could see it clearly.

"And while she doing that, I want to get me a Beauty Salon on the same block. We're trying to see if the bank is going to give us a loan. And if they do, then it's on and popping," my mother said, tightening her grip around my waist.

"Well I'm tellin' you now that my ladies don't need no loan from a bank. I'mma make that happen. I'll support anything positive that comes out of our family." We started to walk down the street toward my truck.

"You mean to tell me that you gon' give us about fifteen thousand to get all this stuff off the ground?" She raised an eyebrow as if she didn't believe that.

"Well, before I leave, I wanna meet with a few of the people that you'll be purchasing these establishments from. You know, the land owners, former business owners, and people of that nature. Then I would like to put everything in place before I leave here. As far as the money go, don't worry about that. Y'all just worry about putting everything together and we'll take it from there."

My aunty's eyes were so bucked that they looked like they were going to pop out of her head and roll down the sidewalk. She even had her mouth open in awe.

"Well dang, how is it that you're younger than me but you're in a better position than I am?"

My mother stepped on to her tippy toes and kissed me on the cheek. "Because he's my baby, that's how."

"Yeah, and he's my big brother," Mary said, opening the door to my truck.

My aunt had inherited my great-grandfather's house. Well, actually it was hers and my mother's, but since my mother was rarely in Jackson, my aunty pretty much considered it hers, and we did, too. It was a nice two story, five bedroom house, with an attic and basement, two bathrooms, and a big kitchen that both my mother and aunty knew how to throw down in.

As soon as we walked through the door, all I could smell were all different kinds of foods. My stomach started growling right away. I took my Jordans off at the door, and walked right into the kitchen, lifting the lids of pots, and sticking my head into the oven until my mother came in laughing and pushed me out of it.

"I got a few church buddies on their way over in about five minutes so y'all better get changed, and prepare to have a lovely meal."

That was all I needed to hear. I made my way into the bathroom, and started to wash my hands when my mother came in and closed the door. She looked at me for a long time before she pushed me to the wall and started kissing my lips with her eyes closed.

"I don't want you all in these country bitchez face when they get over here. Remember that you came to Jackson for me and your sister. Don't make us jealous. You belong to us, not them. You understand that?"

I had to laugh at that a little bit. "Yeah, ma, I hear you loud and clear. I grabbed her into my arms and kissed her on the forehead, and she leaned her head backward, so it ended with me kissing her lips.

I saw right away why my mother gave me that warning. When the friends that my aunty invited over stepped into the house and took their shoes off, they surrounded me right away like I was a piece of meat. I was sitting on the couch, watching a small color television when they came in. A dark-skinned, big-boned sistah with her church hat still on, walked over to the couch and pulled me up by my arm.

"I ain't never seen you around here before, and you sho look good enough to eat."

My mother walked over and took her hand away from me. "Well luckily there is plenty to eat in the kitchen so you don't have to worry about feasting on my baby."

A caramel skinned sistah with curly brownish hair wrapped her arms around me. She felt soft and inviting. I had peeped her body when she came in, and she was stacked. She had a little girl with her that couldn't have been older than four.

"Bless you, little brother. Lord knows you sure are handsome. Is that your truck out there?" She laid her head on my chest like we really knew each other.

My aunty pulled her away from me, but not before she winked her eye, and licked her lips. "Dang, can y'all get off of my nephew?"

Before it was all said and done, I'd hugged three more of the women, and they were all just as aggressive. I could tell that my mother and my sister were upset. When my mother got upset, her yellow face turned a shade of red, and her eyes changed colors. She didn't eat much at dinner, and anytime one of the females tried to flirt with me, she broke it up by telling them that I was already taken.

Later on that night, we were all sitting in living room, watching Soul Food on the little color television, when my sister fell asleep wit her head against my shoulder. I picked her up and asked my mother which one of the rooms she was sleeping in?

"Well, me and her have been sleeping in the guest room at the end of the hall upstairs, but you can take her to the room next to the bathroom up there. Come on, I'll show you."

Before we headed up, Vanessa got up from the couch and stretched her arms over her head, yawning. "Yeah, I guess I'll turn in, too. That way, we can take care of some business in the morning." She leaned down and kissed me on the cheek. "I'll see you in the morning, baby."

I nodded and smiled. I adjusted my sister in my arms and followed my mother up the stairs, where I laid my sister on the bed and covered her with a blanket, after kissing her on the forehead. "Good night, Princess."

I still hadn't figured out where I would be sleeping, so I asked my mother about that. She pulled me by the hand, and led me into the bedroom that her and my sister had been sleeping in since they came to Jackson.

Once we were inside, she closed the door behind us. "I need to talk to you baby," she said, standing in front of me as I sat on the edge of the bed.

The room was bigger than the one we'd placed my sister in. There was a big bed in the middle of it and a dresser along the wall that had a mirror on top of it. "What's on your mind, momma?"

She took my hands and looked me in the eye. "I'm not happy, son. I feel like life is becoming too much for me, and I don't know what to do." I saw the tears rolling down her cheeks. She wiped them away and sniffed through her nose.

I didn't know what to do. This was catching me off guard because she was just smiling and in a good mood. "What's the matter?"

She tilted her head back and inhaled deeply, before blowing it back out. "I'm tired of this everyday pain, baby. I'm tired of being unhappy, of not knowing what to expect tomorrow. There is so much weight on my shoulders that I just don't know what to do." She broke down crying and I pulled her into my arms.

"Tell me what you need for me to do. I don't like to see you breakin' down like this because you know I got you. Everything that I do out in these streets is so I can put you and my little sister in a better position. So tell me what I can do for you?"

She placed her hand on my chest. "I just want you to love me, baby. I need for you to make me know that I am special, and that somebody on this earth loves me for real. I have never had that. I have never had anybody that went above and beyond for me the way that you do. So I know that I got you here," she said as she moved my hand so that it was over her heart.

"But I also need you worse than ever here." She took my hand and put in under her short night gown, opening her legs wide.

I felt her hairless sex lips were as hot as the sun in July. I was strong enough to snatch my hand away from her, and I probably should have, knowing who she was to me. But I didn't. I didn't because I knew I needed to be there for her, and I had already said that there was nothing that I wouldn't do for her, and I meant that. So when she put my hand onto her sex lips, applying pressure until my fingers slipped between them, not penetrating her, but just enough to get trapped between the wet meat on each side that protected her opening, I allowed that to happen.

"I need you so bad, baby," she moaned with tears rolling down her cheeks. "I need you to make me feel like a woman. You'll be the first person to touch me in this way that actually loved me unconditionally. I need you to take this pain away from me." She kissed my neck and opened her legs wider.

"Please, honey."

When she bit into my neck, and moaned into my ear, all I got to thinking about was all of the fantasies that I'd had about her as a kid. She had always been the most beautiful woman in the world to me, and she still was. Her body, as much as I hated to admit it, still drove me crazy, and deep down, a part of me wanted to do exactly what she did.

I pulled her on top of me, and she straddled me with one thick thigh on each side of my stomach. I gripped that fat ass booty, and squeezed it. She moaned into my ear, and kissed my lips, before licking them with her tongue.

"Damn, this that forbidden shit here, baby. I promise that mommy gone make you feel so good. I need you so bad." She lowered her chest to mine, and grinded her pelvis into my already hard dick.

I rubbed all over that booty, then took my fingers from the back and slid them to her super wet pussy. It was so wet that her juices Were oozing out of her and onto my thighs. I could feel her grinding into me, and it was driving me crazy.

She sat up, reached down, and began taking my pants off so fast that, before I knew it, I was naked, laying on my back with her face in between my legs.

"Damn, my baby all grown up," she said, stroking my dick up and down in her little hand. "I need all of this, baby. I don't want you to take it easy on me. Momma need some real love making that will take me away from this pain." She pulled the skin on my dick all the way back, and prepared to put me in her mouth.

In that moment, I don't know what it was but something came over me. I placed my hand on to her forehead, and stopped her. "Wait, ma. I can't let you do that. This ain't right. I think you just real vulnerable right now."

She pushed my hand away from her and sat back on her hunches. The way her legs were spread, I could see right between them. I noted that she had shaved her sex from the last time I had seen it. Her lips were engorged, and opened a little. I could tell that she was very aroused.

"You said that I was your baby, Taurus. You said that you love me, and that you would do anything for me." She swallowed. "Don't you understand how much I need you?"

"Ma, I do, but-"

"But nothing. If you'll fuck all them girls that don't mean nothing to you, and you say you love me more than them, then I should be able to get some of this. I need it more than they do."

And with that, she slid me into her mouth and sucked so hard that my toes curled up. I even let out a little moan like I was a broad or something.

"That's right, baby. Just let momma do her thing," she said, popping me out of her mouth, and then sucking me into it again.

At first, I felt real guilty. But after I felt that heat, and saw the way she got to doing her thing to my piece, I laid on my back and allowed her to drive me crazy. I blocked it out of my mind who she was to me. I figured I'd deal with that whole dilemma in the morning, if even then.

She started pumping her hand up and down my dick real fast, while she kept me in her mouth. "Come for me, baby. Momma want you to come for her, right now."

I couldn't take it no more. I started humping into her mouth, and I had my hand in her long curly hair, and all of it was just too much. I started coming like I never have before. I felt it in my toes first, and the feeling went all the way to the top of my head. I started shaking and she kept on sucking me harder and harder.

When she popped me out of her mouth, she licked up and down my stalk, kissing it. "My baby got a nice big dick. You ready to put all of this in me?" She looked into my eyes seductively.

Before I could even think about it, I pulled her on top of me, and spread her ass. She reached under herself and lined me up, before slowly sliding down my pole. The further down she went, the hotter her pussy got, and the more her walls squeezed the thickness of me. I grabbed her waist and slammed her down. She moaned at the top of her lungs.

"Aw, baby, yes. Finally my baby inside of me. Now just let momma heal herself with you, baby. That's all I need." She rode me nice and slow with her eyes closed and her head tilted back. Tears ran down her cheeks.

I pulled the shoulder straps down on her gown, exposing her brown pretty breasts. There were a few stretch marks that decorated them, but that made me love them even more. I pulled on the nipples before sucking them altogether.

She bounced up and down, with her mouth wide open. "Ah, ah, oh shit, this dick so big. I love it, baby. I love it so much. You finna make momma come all over you." She sped up the pace. "Heal me, Taurus, heal yo momma!"

By that time she was bouncing on me so fiercely that the bed was going haywire. It sounded like there were a bunch of people in there jumping on it. The springs were squeaking like crazy, and the headboard constantly beat into the wall.

"I'm coming, baby. I'm coming," she screamed and dug her fingernails into my chest. I felt her pussy walls clamping and then unclamping all over my pole, and then she fell on top of me.

I flipped her onto her back and put both of her legs on my shoulders. I felt that since we had crossed the line, I might as well enjoy it, and show her how I really get down.

She reached on the side of herself and pulled her inner thighs apart as I drove into her like a bull. "Yes. Just like that. Oh shit, now that's how you fuck, baby. Fuck yo momma just like that. Please, honey!" she exclaimed breathlessly.

I was digging deep into her, bottoming that pussy out. I had already made it up in my mind that this would have been the only time I'd cross these lines with her. I knew that we couldn't keep up something like this, it would have been too dangerous.

I felt her coming under me, which made me speed up the pace and long-stroke her harder. "I love this pussy, momma. I love this pussy!" I closed my eyes as I drilled into her so hard that my abs began to hurt. But the harder I hit that shit, the more she begged me to kill it. The room must've sounded like people were in there fighting. It got to the point that I didn't even care if my sister or Vanessa found out. Forbidden pussy was *that* good.

Chapter 7

I woke up the next morning, with my mother and my sister in my arms. I don't know how that happened, but they were both knocked out and snoring lightly.

Vanessa came into the room and tapped me on the shoulder. That was when I opened my eyes. She held a finger to her lips to shush me, then she pointed at them, and told me to come here.

I climbed out of the bed, after maneuvering my way from under them, and followed her into the hallway. Somehow I had managed to put my boxers back on before I fell asleep, I'm guessing.

When we got into the hallway, she closed the door behind us, and wagged her finger at me in a scolding manner. "Boy, you know how loud you had my sister in there last night? I had to explain to Mary that she had left, and you was in there with somebody else. But I don't think she bought it." She shook her head. " So how long has this been going on?"

I was tired as hell, and a little caught off guard. I didn't feel like explaining myself to her that early in the morning. "Vanessa why are you being so nosey?"

She gave me a look that said I must have lost my mind. "Boy, that's the best you can come up with? I wanna know how long y'all been fucking. I mean I ain't downing it or nothing. To be honest, it's hot to me. I'm just curious."

I shrugged my shoulders after yawning into my hand. "That was the first and last time. She needed me, and I'll do anything for my mother. Pointblank, period."

She kissed me on the cheek. "That's what's up. I'm about to go make breakfast. I'll come wake y'all up in about an hour." She pulled open my boxers and looked down into them. "Now I see why she was in there screaming. Mystery solved."

Later that day, I took them on a shopping spree at Jackson City Mall. I let them pick out whatever they wanted. They had so many bags in their hands that I wound up carrying a few.

Before we left the mall, I bought all three of them diamond tennis bracelets with the matching pink lemonade diamond ear rings.

My mother held my hand the whole time and barely left my sight. She kept on laying her head on my shoulder and telling me how much she loved me, and appreciated me.

We met with a few business men that were overseers of the property my mother and aunty wanted to acquire to set their businesses on. It didn't take long for us to close those deals. Money talked, and it was that simple.

On the night that I left Jackson, my mother pulled me to the side, and into the upstairs bedroom, closing the door.

"Taurus, I love you, and I will never forget what you did for me for as long as I live. I know we can't do that all the time, but when I need you, just say that you'll make that trip out here for me. And if you will, I know I can be strong and hold on until things get better. Can you promise me that?"

I kissed her on the forehead. "I owe you more than this life, momma. You gave me this body, so whenever you need me in any way, I'll be here. For now, get your business up and running, and don't worry about nothing. You got all my contact information and you are my first priority for the rest of my life." I grabbed her and hugged her tightly, while she cried on my chest.

Before I left, I hit her with ten gees, and gave my sister and aunty five a piece.

***

When I got back to Memphis, Tywain met me at Boogaloo's, which was a hood sub joint. We met in the parking lot. It was real gloomy outside and kind of cold. It looked like it was either going to rain or snow. As soon as I got out of the whip, he hugged me.

"Yo, it's been crazy over the last few days, boss. Muhfuckas been getting killed left and right."

We got into my truck. "Anybody we know?"

He shook his head. "Nah, just some off-brand Crip niggaz. Them and the Asian Bloodz beefing like crazy. But the more they focus in on that war shit, the easier it'll be for us to keep getting money. And, my nigga, we getting cash muthafucking money!" He had a grin on his face so wide that I thought his jaws were gonna get stretch marks. Even though I had the shit that had took place with my mother heavy on my mind, hearing about money changed my mind real quick. Besides, what was done, was done. I ain't regret one bit of it.

"Yo the lil homies clocking paper, too. They taking being Comma Kids serious. All three trap houses sold out in less than two days. I hit they ass with another shipment, and lil bro nem damn near through already." He slapped his hands together and rubbed them. "I'm ready to kick this shit off with The Rebirth, mane. I know once muhfuckas get a load of that, we about to blow up!"

He started getting me geeked up. "Nigga we gotta make that shit happen this weekend. I was thinking that we throw a big party for all of the heroin addicts in the Mound, or on that side of town period, and we'll cater it with The Rebirth. Once they get a load of our shit, that's gone be all she wrote, trust me."

Tywain frowned. "I thought we was about to bumrush some shit. Since when did you come up with this plan?"

"I got to thinking when I was out there with my mother and shit. I wouldn't want no nigga forcing her to no ground and putting that poison in her. If a muhfucka gone fuck with The Rebirth, they gone do that shit all on they on. We ain't gotta force the money to come, it's gone come anyway. The last thing we need is a bunch of enemies like Hood Rich nem'. If it was up to me, I'd find another way to get rich, but this just the hand we've been dealt. So we gotta finesse this shit and turn it into something worthy."

"Damn, nigga, you only been gone a few days. You done came up with all of this?" He started laughing. "Yo, I'm wit you no matter what you wanna do." He took a cigarette out and lit it. "How your moms doing?"

I nodded. "She good, my lil sister is, too. My mother about to open her own salon. It's a start. After her first business, ain't no telling where things will go. I'm just glad that my lil sister got her as a role model."

"Before I forget, I saw Princess the other day with some yellow ass female. She told me that when I saw you to tell you to get up with her since you ain't answering your phone or been on Facebook."

I waved him off. "I'll get up wit her in a minute. I probably gotta hit her hand wit some more of that tropical shit. She ain't say nothing to you about it?"

He shook his head. "Nall, but she did say that nigga Juice wanna holler at you in person. I don't know if I'd do that though."

"Why not?" I asked, lowering my window. I hated the smell of cigarettes, especially when the smoke circulated around in the car. I raised my window back up and lowered his a crack so the smoke could escape without going past me.

"Because that nigga said he was gon' kill you. I don't give a fuck if he your blood brother or not. If a nigga say he gone kill you, then you take that shit serious. From that point on, I wouldn't have shit to do with him. I'd wait until the first day he touched down and knock his head off. I mean, noodles all over the concrete."

I curled my lip at that. I didn't know how I really felt about him talking about whacking my brother, but I knew he meant well and just cared about me. "Yo, one thing about Juice, that nigga always expose his hand. So if I went out there to see him, he wouldn't be able to hide his true intentions. Let me think about that later, though. Right now, we got too much shit in rotation to be worried about what this nigga finna do. Let's get this money."

"I couldn't have said it better."

***

That weekend, we threw a dope party in Orange Mound, and advertised the fact that we would be giving away blows for free. We promised food, drinks, and as much dope as you could buy.

Before the party, we'd hit the cops that patrolled the area with a gee a piece, and they gave us until two in the morning to do what we needed to do. So we started the party at nine that night.

We made it a pajama party, but most of the fiends came wearing robes, and even so, they were searched at the door thoroughly, the women as well. We didn't want no drama at this party. All we wanted was as many customers at the end as possible. I don't know how Pooky did it, but it wasn't later than nine thirty when the whole backyard and house was filled with addicts. I mean, it had to be at least three hundred people there, and I knew there were more corning.

I was in the living room, surveying everything, when Tywain

came up to me in a frenzy. "Yo, this shit is getting crazy, boss. Ain't no way all of these people about to fit up in here, and these muhfuckas stank." He curled his nose and pinched it closed with his fingers.

The more I looked around, the more I started to see that he was right. "You know what? This what we gon' do. We gon' have these muhfuckas line up, and we gon' give every one of them a shot of The Rebirth until we trick off an entire kilo. By that time, the line should have made it back to the beginning, and the muhfuckas that we started with will be paying for it."

That was exactly what we did. It took us three hours to give everybody their first dose. I made sure that I told them that if the next time I saw them they had some body new with them that used, I'd give them another dose for free. It was crazy because it was like all of the fiends were finding other fiends. It got to the point that we wound up using up a kilo and a half. But we served over two thousand people, and gave them our contact information.

That was the night that Tywain said since our lil homies were calling themselves Comma Kids, we would be referred to as the Comma Kings.

The next morning we hit the ground running, and our phones were ringing like crazy.

I knocked on Princess' door later the next night. She answered the door, saw that it was me, and ran right into my arms. "Taurus, I thought that something happened to you." She broke into a fit of tears. "They found my brother's body. They found him buried in a damn corn field. Somebody had blew his head off." She whimpered and fell against me.

I felt a chill go down my spine. "When did this happen?"

I asked, stroking her back.

"Yesterday morning. I guess some old farmer stumbled across his body as he was plowing his field. "She slumped to the carpet. What am I going to do?"

I knelt down, picked her up some, and wrapped her into my arms. "I got you. Whatever you need, just let me know."

"Thank you. You know your brother has been blowing me up. He wanna talk to you real bad. He says that he thinks he knows who killed my brother, but he'll only tell you because it's somebody you might know. That crushed my soul. That's my brother and he won't even tell me."

I was beginning to see why Juice wanted to see me so bad. The cat was out of the bag, and he was worried about what I'd do now that it was. My heart started to beat faster.

"Princess, was there anybody else found?"

She nodded, "Yeah, some white boy. I don't know how him and my brother got buried together, but somehow they did. It was all over Facebook. I'm surprised you ain't know about this."

I shook my head. I was starting to panic. "I ain't even had my phone on because I was chilling with my mother and sister out in Jackson." I just knew that if this shit was all over Facebook, I'd be getting a call from Serge or

Russell soon. I didn't know how I would face them. I turned on my phone and got on Facebook. Sure enough, I had so many messages from Nastia that it wasn't funny. As soon as she knew that I was logged on, she sent me a message asking me where had I been.

"I need help burying him. I don't have the money. They're talking about a minimum of seven thousand." She lowered her head. "What am I going to do?"

I typed Nastia that I would meet with her in an hour.

"I already told you that I had you. Don't worry about the expenses. I got you. You just get everything together, and I'll handle the rest."

She hugged me tightly. "I love you so much, Taurus. What would I do without you?"

As soon as my truck pulled into the parking lot of Boogaloo's, Nastia damn near ran up to it and ogled the lever of the passenger's door handle before getting in. "Taurus, my father found my brother's body along with that other black dude's. There is going to be trouble." Her hair was pulled all the way back. She didn't have a lick of make up on. I could tell that she was stressed. "Why haven't you been answering your phone?"

I shook my head and turned down the R. Kelly record that played through my speakers. "Yo, I iust been handling a lot of business. I ain't have my phone on at all."

She got irritated. "I better not find out that you were laid up with some hoochie or whatever while I've been out here trying to figure out a way to throw my father off of your scent. If he finds out that you've had anything to do with my kidnap, he's going to kill you. That, I can promise."

I curled my upper lip. I wasn' t about to just let nobody just kill me and not do anything about it. I knew she feared her father, and to a certain degree, I feared his power, not him as a man. But I was tired of feeling some type of say about the whole situation. "Nastia, you can quit hollering that killing me shit. Now I respect your father, but I ain't gon' just sit back and let nobody kill me. We know I ain't have shit to do with you and your brother being snatched up. I was the one that made sure you got home safe and sound."

"I know that, Taurus, but what will he think if he connects the dots? What's to stop him from overthinking things and going over the deep end?"

"You, baby." I reached over and squeezed her slim thigh. "Your father isn't crazy enough to think that you would be dealing wit yo kidnapper. He gotta trust you to a certain extent."

She shrugged her shoulders. "I don't know. I mean, I guess. I just don't understand why you weren't answering your phone. I mean, I'm trying to do everything that I can for you to show you that I'm down for you more than anybody else. All I ask in return is that you make me your girl." She frowned, and lowered her head.

Here I was trying to figure out how I was going to mentally manipulate her father into believing that I had nothing to do with his daughter's kidnapping, and she was sitting in my truck trying to figure out if she was my girl or not. Women were so hard to deal with at times. I guess she really didn't realize that my life was on the line. And if she did, she didn't take it serious. A part of me wanted to kick her out of my truck because she was giving me a headache. But had I done that, I would for sure be in an all-out war with a powerful Russian, not to mention, I would lose my connection. So I had to play things extremely strategic. Her emotions were out of whack, so I had to prey on them.

I grabbed her by her ponytail roughly, and kissed her lips, before sucking all over them with an occasional bite here and there. "You are my girl. You my baby. Don't you forget that shit. I don't give a fuck whether my phone is off or on. That don't change your position. Do you understand that?"

She blinked her bright blue eyes a few times before smiling, and wrapping her arms around my neck. "You're driving me crazy, Taurus. I'm serious. I am really starting to go insane because of you." She kissed my lips softly. "Please don't ever leave me for one of those black girls out there. I mean, I know that my skin is not as nice as theirs, but I will do everything that I can to keep you happy."

Now she was talking like I needed her to talk. I needed to stay in her head. As long as I had her head, I would be able to control the game, a game that me and my right hand man was winning in because of her connections.

"Baby, you keep me very happy." I rubbed her pussy mound through her jeans. "Baby, I need you to handle this shit wit yo old man. I'm gone sit down wit him and everything, but at the end of the day I need for you to keep his ear because you're his little girl."

She blushed, "I know that." She squeezed my bicep. "So what do you want me to do?"

"When we sit down, all I want you to do is follow my lead."

***

That night, me and Tywain sat down with her father at one of his houses in Burbank. His security team led us down a stairwell that took us into a big board room. He sat at the head of the table and told us to have a seat. The first thing I noticed when I sat down was that there was a big plastic ball sitting in front of him. I couldn't really tell what it was, but I found it odd to be there.

Nastia sat at the table at her father's right side, Russell sat at his left, and the rest of the people that sat at the table looked Russian, and they were all heavily armed with menacing scowls on their faces.

I found it odd that Serge didn't shake my hand when I first came into the room. Neither did Russell.

"Okay, it's time we begin this meeting," Serge began, before taking a sip of a white fluid in a glass. I figured it to be Vodka, but then again, I wasn't sure. I just knew he was usually drinking Vodka whenever I saw him for the most part. "As you all know, my son's body was exhumed from a cornfield not three days ago. The cause of his death was multiple gun shot wounds to the body and head. This does not make me happy."

I looked over to Tywain, and he was looking directly at Serge, giving him his full undivided attention. I tried to get ahold of myself, but my nerves were getting the best of me. I felt like Serge had called the meeting for a particular reason.

"I find it odd that my son was murdered and my daughter was not. I know the kinds of enemies that I have, and when they kill one, they kill all." He took the plastic wrapped ball in front of him and slammed it on the table. It made a loud thumping sound. "Nothing made sense to me until I had this brought to my attention."

He peeled away the wrapping of the plastic in a frenzy. The more plastic he peeled away, the more I started to get sick to my stomach, especially when he got finished and I saw that it was Pac Man's head. He held it in the air by his dreads.

"This is somebody that you know, is it not?" he asked, looking from Tywain to me.

Tywain shrugged his shoulders. "Yeah, I know that nigga. I seen him around town a few times, but I never fucked with him like that. That nigga's a fiend, and I don't fuck wit dope fiends."

Serge stood up holding the head by the dreads. He started to walk around the table, stopping behind my chair. "From what I hear, this is your brother's best friend. So tell me, Taurus, why would your brother's best friend be buried in the same grave as my son?"

I tried my best to remain calm, but every eye in the room was looking at me. The Russian bodyguards looked like they wanted to kill me, and they were just waiting on the order from Serge. "Yo, I don't know why they would be buried in the same grave. I didn't fuck wit dude like that. That's my brother's guy, and from as far as I know, he had plenty enemies. Ain't no telling what happened to him and your son."

Serge busted out laughing. "What do you think, that I'm some kind of an idiot. Haven't you ever heard the saying that wherever there is smoke, there is a fire."

"Yeah."

He leaned into my ear so close that his lips grazed my skin. "Well right now you are smoking, and I'm seconds away from lighting you on fire." He stood up. "I never trusted you from the first day I met you. I knew you had an agenda." He snapped his fingers, and his gunmen stood up. "I want you to take him out back, chop his head off, and bring it to me. Bury his body in the same grave they pulled my son from. An eye for an eye."

They rushed over to pull me from my chair. I reached into

the small of my back and came up with my .9 millimeter. I was ready to blow some muhfuckas heads off. I wasn't going out like no coward.

"Wait! Dad, I can't let you do this. I gotta tell you the truth. Brad and that guy were doing Meth together, and that guy tried to rob us. After he took all of our cash, he took me into the house where I showed him where the stashes were. Brad had previously refused, so I guess that made him angry and before I could beg him not to do it, Brad tried to attack him. That's when the guy killed him, and then the Mexican guy that I told you about killed him and took me hostage. He said that the other guy was greedy, and he couldn't trust him. That's all I know."

All of the Russian men had surrounded me. If not for Serge putting his hand up to stop them, I would have been in their backyard, dead.

He went around and knelt in front of his daughter, looking up into her eyes. "Baby, I need for you to tell me that this man did not have anything to do with your abduction. Promise me on the love that we have for each other."

Nastia looked down on him and put both of her hands onto his shoulders. "This is the man that saved me from it all. If not for him, I would have been dead, and probably buried in the same grave with Brad. He is my friend now, and you should not hurt him because he saved me, your only daughter."

Serge stayed down on one knee looking at her for a long time. He took a deep breath, and exhaled. "Okay then, if you say so, sweetheart." He stood up and turned to me. "You can go. But if I ever am able to prove that you had something to do with this kidnapping, I will not be so kind to you. I will repay you an eye for an eye."

Tywain stood up and we shot out of there as fast as we could.

Chapter 8

I waited two months before I went to see Juice. I didn't feel like putting up with him for a little while. I tried to keep my mind focused on our many business ventures, and getting The Rebirth up and running powerfully. We already had damn near the entire city shooting our poison. It had gotten so good that we were going through about five kilos a day. Now we sold our product in no bigger quantities than a dime bag. We never sold weight because we wanted to maximize our profits.

The Rebirth had me seeing more money than I ever had in my whole entire life. I mean, it was coming in bundles. So much so that we had to find a way to start turning it over so that Uncle Sam got his cut. I think the correct term for it was called money laundering.

We got to hitting up local businesses in the neighborhood, and having them put twenty and thirty thousand into their back accounts every other week, or whenever they usually made deposits. In exchange for their assistance, we'd give them a thousand dollars cash or, depending on the owner, a nice portion of The Rebirth. By that time, there were so many people doing the drug that most of the business owners were hooked, so instead of them taking our cash, they took the product happily.

It was around this same time that Nastia hooked me up with a few Swiss accounts. So after the establishments in our hood would launder the money for us, we'd wire it to our Swiss accounts. She laced me a whole lot with the corporate side of the game. Fucking with that white girl had me thinking all the way outside of the box.

Even though we were pretty much tearing down the community on one hand, on the other, I was helping to get more community centers and youth programs into our hoods. We got a few play grounds built up, and had a few buildings renovated and turned into community centers and after school programs. I didn't have it all figured out, all I knew was that I wanted to take some of the evil out of our money and make it more godly. I knew that sounded kinda fucked up, but like I said, I didn't have it all figured out yet.

Tywain flat out acted like he didn't give a fuck. I mean, he would see kids starving, or dirty as hell, and would walk right past them. I couldn't do that. I had to take them shopping, and then out for a bite to eat. I had a few buildings around town where I made sure kids could go to get three meals a day. Not no little ass meals either. I'm talking full course meals, where they could burp.

We decided to use a play out of Hood Rich's playbook, where we made sure that anybody that used our product and was so dependent on it that they didn't feed their children, we took their Food Share cards and turned it into The Rebirth for them. Then with the money on the Food Share cards, we'd converted that into food for them and put it back into their homes so that their kids could eat every day. We held all of their identifications, and allowed them to cash their checks with us. We also had a bank account set up at this Credit Union that was run by one of our customers, where any time one of our users got paid, their funds were direct deposited into that account.

If they used this system, for every one hundred dollars they spent with us, we added fifty to the sale. We paid their rents with this same account, and took care of the things that were supposed to be taking care of. My whole thing was that I didn't want the kids to suffer, and as far as I could control, they didn't. If it was found out that someone was neglecting their kids, or not paying their bills, they were cut off from The Rebirth, and anybody caught buying or sharing our Rebirth with them was also cut off. I took that shit very serious, and my right hand man did not.

On the day I went to see Juice, I had just finished coming from a meeting where I had gotten it approved for the city to build two new playgrounds. They had already opened three new Boys and Girls Clubs because I'd funded them, so I was feeling good about myself.

As soon as Juice came into the visiting room, the first thing I noted was that he had gained some weight, and looked like he'd been lifting a lot of iron. I made sure I worked out like crazy every single day as well, so I wasn't intimidated. I was simply surprised because the last time I'd seen him he'd been so skinny.

He walked over to the table and sat down. "You can't let that bitch find out that I killed her brother. Right now I'm working on something with her, and I can't afford for it to go south. You feel me?" he asked, looking at the floor instead of me.

I rolled my head around on my shoulders. I got to feeling irritated immediately. "Bro, don't you know the last thing you said to me was that you was gone kill me when you catch me? Now you givin' me orders and shit. What's up wit you?" I asked mugging the shit out of him.

He raised his head and frowned. "Nigga, I remember, and I ain't say I changed my mind either. I'm just telling you to keep yo mouth shut, seeing as you got a problem wit that."

"What the fuck you talking about, Juice? When did I open my mouth against anything?"

"I'm sittin' in this prison, ain't I? I mean, I ain't put myself here." He mugged me and curled his upper lip like he was disgusted with by presence.

I got super irritated. "I keep tellin' yo stupid ass that you was makin' some fucked up decisions. You could have got our mother and Marykilled over some shit they ain't have no part of. You act like you don't give a fuck about them. "

"Act? Nigga, I told you a long time ago that I don't. I don't understand how you can't get that shit through your big ass head. Fuck them! If you ain't my father, then fuck you. When I get home, trust me, Taurus, I'm gon' fuck you over, nigga." He adjusted himself in the chair. "You think I give a fuck about who that bitch was? You think I gave a fuck about her punk ass brother that got bagged?" He sucked his teeth loudly. "Nigga, I know you bagged Gotto, and I don't even give a fuck about that. "

That last comment sent a chill down my spine. I felt my heart beating fast just thinking back on what he said about my mother and sister. I felt like hitting him in his shit. "I see being in here ain't help you grow up none. You still a stupid ass, doped out kid. You don't give a fuck about nobody other than yourself, never have."

"Bitch nigga, never have, and never will." He leaned forward into my face. "When I get out of this muthafucka, I'm gone show you the meaning of everything I'm saying. I can't wait. Lord knows, I can't wait. I'm telling you now that you better have all of yo shit together, because if you don't, you gone be sorry. That's my word."

I was quiet for a long time. My heart was beating so fast that I didn't know what to do. I had visions on stealing off of him and knocking him out again, like I did when we were kids. I hated my brother in that moment. I felt like I could kill him and have no remorse.

"Now, when you leave out this muhfucka, I want you to make sure you keep yo mouth closed. Don't turn bitch. Let me knock out the rest of this time, and when I get out, we gone meet in the streets and slug it out like real gees. There can only be one prodigal son in the family, and that's me. I'm knockin' that head off yo shoulders, nigga. I promise that on my father's blood."

I nodded. "You know what, Juice, I'm gon' kill you. As much as I know I'm supposed to love you, and be my brother's keeper, it's like I was born to kill both of you nothin' ass niggas. I can't wait to you get out, because when you do, I'm gone body you in cold blood, and I put that on my mother's blood."

"Nigga, fuck that bitc-"

Before he could even finish the insult, I hit him in his mouth so hard that he fell out of the chair. I jumped on top of him and started to rain down fists into his face again and again until the guards pulled me off of him. "Fuck nigga, don't you ever disrespect my mother like that," I yelled, kicking my legs and trying to get back at him, but they were holding me by the arms three deep.

Juice sat on the floor with a mouth full of blood laughing like a mental patient. "Yeah, bitch nigga. I'll be home soon. I just might bag that bitch, too. The throne is mine. You better hope they kill yo ass before I do, and beware of that red rag." He opened his mouth wide and laughed at the top of his lungs as the guards carried him out with blood and mucus dripping off his chin in thick ropes.

They gave me a five thousand dollar ticket and banned me from the prison, but I didn't give a fuck. Not only had that nigga threatened my life, but now he made it seem like my mother was in jeopardy as well. That shit didn't sit right with me. I knew in that moment that I was going to kill him. I yearned to do it. I needed to do it. That night I went to where we'd poured Gotto's ashes and I sat back smiling collecting my thoughts.

The next morning, we ran through Black Haven. Tywain had decided that since we went the nice route with the Orange Mound, he should be able to handle Black Haven in any way that he wanted. So he took the Hood Rich and Meech approach. He had our troops kick in doors and force The Rebirth into the systems of any adults that were present. He even hit up some older teens.

It seemed like the more money he made, the crazier he became. I sat back and watched while they kicked in the first apartment door, with guns drawn, and then our troops filed into it. All I could hear was a bunch of screaming. When two children ran out of the place with tears in their eyes, I felt my stomach turn. It took two hours before all of the buildings were run through and injected.

Shakia went into labor two weeks later. Her mother had hit me up on Facebook, letting me know. That pissed me off because no matter what kinds of differences we had, I had done my thing to hold her down during the whole pregnancy. I didn't hit the pussy, but I was still there for her in every other way.

When I got there, her mother, Shaneeta, was in the waiting room pacing back and forth. As soon as she saw me, she ran into my arms and hugged me super tight. Then she took a step back and smacked me on the chest. "What took you so long to get here? I texted yo ass three hours ago," she said as she walked around me and gave Tywain a hug.

"We was tied up on some business in Orange Mound. As soon

as I got your text, I shot over here, though. I just ain't have my phone on me," I said, rubbing my chest, and frowning.

"Yeah, ma, he ain't lying. Some niggas tried to pull some bullshit on one of the traps over there, but everything situated now, so it's good."

She wrapped her arm around my waist. "I don't know why they ain't letting me back there with her. I hope everything is okay."

I was confused, "Wait, why wouldn't it be?"

Just as I asked that question, one of the nurses came out of the room that Shakia was in and asked which one of us was the father?

I raised my hand, "That would be me."

The skinny white woman waved me over to follow her, and I did. "She's doing okay. She's actually ready to give birth. She kept on asking if the father was here yet, and saying that she didn't want anybody else in the room other than you."

We stopped in the hallway and she showed me how to wash my arms and hands. Then she handed me a set of scrubs and told me I could change in the bathroom. It took me all.of five minutes to do, and then I was back in the hallway staring at her.

"Okay, now when you go in, you're probably gonna wanna stay by her head, and away from the birthing area."

I raised my eyebrow confused. "What do you mean birthing area?"

She smiled, "I mean her vagina. Right now it's not looking like you're accustomed to it looking. Trust me, if you have any feelings for her, and you want to carryon in a sexual relationship with her, you will not look down at her area during this process. Just trust me on that," she said, looking me straight in the eyes.

"Well, what if I don't want any of those things with her anyway?" Because I didn't. I already knew that I would never lay down with her again. I didn't want a relationship with her, all I wanted to do was co-parent. That was it.

At first she looked confused, and then she shrugged her shoulders. "Okay then, if that's the case." She waved for me to follow her. When we got outside of Shakia's room, the nurse opened the door, and kind of pushed me in.

"Doctor, this is the father. Father, you enjoy the show." She rolled her eyes and walked off.

The doctor was assisted by a heavyset black nurse with glasses on her face. "Baby, do you wanna support her from my end, or do you want to go up there and hold her hand, and take care of her?"

I didn't know how I was supposed to support her from the doctor's end, so I told her that I would support Shakia from up top. Her feet were already in stirrups, and they had a blue sheet draped across her waist. As soon as I got close enough for her to touch me she grabbed at my hand until it was in her embrace.

"Taurus, I'm so scared. Thank you for being here. It really means a lot to me." She laid her head back on the pillow and started to do her breathing exercises that they had taught us in class.

I did the best I could to coach her along. About an hour later, the baby started to crown. I urged her to push, and the more she did, the harder she squeezed my hand, until I was about ready to let her hand go. I know that was real pussy, but until a man allows a woman to hold his hand while she's giving birth, he couldn't begin to understand how that pain feels. I'm pretty sure the women would say that it doesn't compare to the pain that's going on between their legs.

Shakia gave birth to a six-pound eleven-ounce little boy. The whole time I had been preparing for her to have a girl, and it turned out to be a boy. She named him Tremarion, and gave him my middle name, Jahrome. He came out screaming and wiggling his little legs. After they cleaned him up thoroughly , the doctor handed him to Shakia, and she handed him directly to me.

I held him in my arms and looked down at his face. He already had real deep dimples just like me, and his facial shape was that of mine. His hair was very curly, and his skin complexion was a little light, but I was always told that babies got their real color over time.

"How do you feel, Taurus? Do you feel any connection to him?" Shakia asked, looking like she'd just run a marathon.

I couldn't stop my heart from beating so fast. As I looked down at the baby, I started to feel all kinds of emotions. I felt love for him. I felt like I needed to protect him. I felt like I needed to give him the best life possible, and on top of that, I felt like he was mine. Before I even knew it I had tears in my eyes.

"Yeah, I feel a connection. I gotta take care of him and make sure he straight at all times."

Tywain came in and I handed my son to him. He lifted him in the air, and smiled. "He definitely got that big ass head. That's for sure." He pulled him down and kissed him on the forehead. "You gon' forever be good, lil homie. Yo Pops got stupid bread, and we gettin' more every single day. I'm yo uncle, and I'll kill a nigga dead over you. Remember that."

Shaneeta looked at him like he had lost his mind. "Boy, can you hand me my grandbaby before you put him in a drive by already? Damn! He ain't even a hour old, and already you trying to turn him into a thug." She took the baby from him and wrapped him in her arms. "I love you so much, grandbaby. Grandma gon' spoil you to death."

Shakia reached and grabbed my hand, and for the first time in a long time, I felt a spark from her. I leaned down and kissed her on the forehead, and then the lips.

"I love you, Taurus. I swear to God I do."

"I know, baby, and what's crazy is that I love you, too. Thank you for bringin' my son into this world."

She nodded and laid her head back on the pillow as she closed her eyes.

Before I could even enjoy my son, my phone vibrated, and a text came through from Gary saying that he needed our assistance right away, and to meet him at Boogaloo's.

Chapter 9

As soon as we got there, Gary jumped out of his Denali, walked over to my truck, and got in the back. "Yo, it's time to splash some niggas. Muhfuckas thinking that since we getting money now, we ain't bout that life. I'm ready to body some niggas, no lie."

Tywain turned around in his seat. "Lil homie, what's the biz, my nigga?"

"It's this fuck crew that hustle around the Mound that's going around harassing our customers, and telling them that if they catch them copping from us, they gone knock they head off. These niggas like ten deep. They push that tar shit. Before we took over with The Rebirth, they was out here eating. Now muhfuckas starving, and they think they about to run the money away." He took out a fat ass .44 desert eagle, and cocked it. "I ain't always been no Trap star. Yo, I been killing niggas since I learned how to load a banger. I'm ready to wet some shit."

Tywain got to nodding his head real hard. "Hell yeah, me too. It's been a while since I bodied a nigga. I miss that shit. Don't you Taurus?"

I still had my lil man on my mind. I was thinking about how he felt in my arms. This must've been the feeling DJ Khaled talked about when he spoke about his son, Asad. "Nigga, we having money now, so we ain't even gotta get our hands dirty."

Tywain waved me off. "Fuck that! This money don't mean shit. I wanna kill somethin', and nigga you rolling wit me. Now who head we knocking off lil homie?"

"One of the niggas name is Trouble. He a lil short stocky nigga, and his right hand man name Chaka. Even though that nigga Chaka don't be on shit like that, I say he guilty by association. I wanna wet both of them niggas, and kill they whole crew. That way we ain't gotta worry about them no more."

"Shid, I'm wit it. Where these niggas hang at?" Tywain asked, lighting a blunt and passing it to Gary.

"They stay at this lil duplex right next to the corner store over on Townsend. They niggas so stupid that they keep they trap door wide open so they can hear the music outside while they on the porch." He shook his head. "I wanna massacre these niggas."

Tywain pulled at the hairs on his chin. "Yo, you real quiet over there, Taurus. What's on yo mind?"

"Shit, if we gone move on these fuck niggas, let's make a real statement. I got some shit on my chest I need to get off anyway."

He nodded.

"When you think is the best time to handle shit. Like what's going on right now?"

He shrugged his shoulders. "I don't know, let's roll through and just see what they doing."

I started up my truck just as Tywain passed me the blunt and sat his Mach .90 on his lap with the extended clip. It held a hundred fifty shots in the magazine. I took my tech .9 and did the same. I really didn't wanna get in no drawn out beef, so if it was best to kill these niggas off, then I wanted to make sure they were shot the fuck up, and dead.

We turned on to their block, and immediately I started to feel some type of way because the first thing I noted was that there were little girls on one side of the street jumping double dutch. It had to be about ten of them, and they couldn't have been any older than ten years old. They looked happy and like they were having a good time. On the porch of their house, I could see two older ladies chatting with each other. "Yo, what side of the street these niggas stay on?" I asked, imagining one of the little girls being my sister, Mary.

Gary pointed out of my window toward the other side of the street. I sighed in relief. "They house at the end of the street, right next to the store down there. Just keeping rolling and you'll see it."

The block had somebody on damn near every porch. I had a bad feeling about this move. The closer we got to their house, it was like the more the sun came from behind the clouds. At first, it looked like it was going to rain, but then the clouds vanished, and the temperature rose.

As I got to the end of the block, I saw a porch full of niggas. They had to be about thirty deep. Most of them had their shirts off, and fitted hats on. The ones that didn't, had dreads. All of them were covered in tattoos. I even made out a few females in the pack.

"Yo, that's them niggas right there. Let's wet they ass." Gary said, switching to the other seat in the back and rolling down the window, preparing to stick his gun out of it.

" Nigga, you done lost yo muthafuckin' mind. We ain't finna do that shit in my truck." I mugged him.

"Damn, I ain't even think about that," he said, sitting back and shaking his head.

"That's why you don't need to do no muhfuckin' thinking. Let us think for you. That's how you got to where you at right now."

He curled his upper lip.

As we rode past the porch full of niggas, they mugged the shit out of my truck, and one of them threw his arms up.

"That's that nigga Chaka right there. Bitch ass nigga."

I eyed him, and smiled to myself. If at first I didn't want to get on no bullshit, that lil intimidation shit he did flipped a switch in me. "I'm finna park this muhfucka a few blocks down and we gone go handle these niggas. I feel like getting a lil blood on my hands anyway."

"That's what I'm talking about," Tywain said taking off his black Polo shirt, and ripping it up. "We ain't been in the news' headlines in a long time." He laughed, and continued to rip up the shirt.

Instead of us going right back. We stopped at Jack in the Box and fed our stomachs. I was hungry as hell, and so were the homies. I honestly think, though, that a part of me used the fact that we were all hungry to buy time. It was already starting to get dark when we first pulled away from them. The sun had come from behind the clouds, only to set, which was a good thing. I didn't really wanna pull a move in broad day light. I thought that it would be stupid, and a little careless on our parts.

We were having money now, so every move had to be thought all the way through. Not to mention, I hoped those little girls had gone into their houses. I ain't want them to witness what we were about to do. And I wasn't saying that because I feared one of them pointing us out to the cops. Nall, I was hoping they didn't see shit that would fuck them up for the long haul.

After we ate, I parked my truck, and we took alleys all the way back to where Chaka and Trouble trapped. We stopped in their backyard and put the black shirt pieces that Tywain had made out of his shirt around our faces.

From their backyard, we could still hear them out on the porch, just as loud as ever.

"Lets go kill these fuck niggas. I'm letting you niggas know now that I'm hitting everthing in sight. That go for bitchez and all," Tywain said holding his Mach up by his chin.

Gary shrugged his shoulders. "Shid, that's what I'm finna do."

As he said that, their back door opened up, and we scattered. There was an abandoned car in their backyard, so we ran and hid on the side of it. I looked out and saw a dude carrying two black garbage bags in his hands.

Tywain nodded at me, and I could see his eyes lower. "Watch this shit." He got up and slowly snuck behind the dude, until he was right on him. Then he stood up and wrapped his arm around his neck from the back, choking him with all of his might.

Tywain fell to the ground with him, still choking. I saw the dude's feet kicking in a frenzy. The more they kicked the harder Tywain squeezed until he stopped kicking, only then did Tywain stand up.

"Come on, Taurus, you go around the side of the house and me and Gary gone go in through the back door. As you see they ass running out, you body they ass. No mercy."

I nodded and waited for them to go into the back door. As soon as they did, I jogged around to the side of the house. I looked up ahead and could see that there was still a few people standing in front of the house. I crept all the way near the front and waited until I heard gun shots. As soon as I did, I ran to the front of the house, and came up to the side of the porch. I saw five dudes and two females.

I raised my Tech and pulled the trigger, aiming at the dude closest to me.

Taa!t Taat! Taat! Taat! The Tech jumped in my hands as I saw his face split down the middle. A Mexican looking female next to him started to scream. I grabbed her by the hair, threw her to the ground, and hit up the dude that stood behind her. I popped him three times in the forehead. His blood splashed on the girl that was screaming on the ground. One dude tried to jump over the porch on the other side, but before he could, I hit him six times in the back. He jumped and landed on his neck. Two more females fell to the ground and started screaming at the top of their lungs. I heard shots going off in the house. I could tell they were getting closer toward the front of the house.

I counted about five females on the porch, and one other dude that was laid on his stomach trying to cover his head. I walked over to him and popped him twice in the back of the head. I grabbed the females up and pushed them toward the backyard.

"Get. Go. Now," I said through clenched teeth while firing in the air. They took off running at full speed.

I heard more gunfire erupt inside the house, and then the door flew open, and a young girl about the age of sixteen ran into my arms. I'll never forget her face. She had a really big mole on the side of her nose, right on her left cheek. Her eyes were brown, and her hair was curly.

When she ran into my arms, the first thing she did was scream, " Please don't kill me. Please. I'm only fifteen years old."

I looked over her shoulder back into the house. I knew that Tywain and Gary had to be on their way out. I disguised my voice. "I'm gon' let you go, but if anybody ask you why this happened to them, you tell them that nobody fucks over Jerry Walker and lives to tell about it. You got that?"

She nodded her head. "Yes."

"Okay, now go." Hurry up."

That night, I had all sorts of nightmares. It had been a while since I'd killed somebody, and for me, the nightmares always came directly afterwards. I saw all kinds of spirits chasing me and asking me why I killed them. I woke up in a cold sweat, and looked at the clock, noting that it was three in the morning. I decided to take a drive.

After rolling around the city for about an hour, I wound up at Princess's crib. I had already looked on my phone and saw that she was up and on Facebook. I typed that I was on my way to her crib, and she said it was cool.

When I got there, she opened the door with a pink robe on. I pulled her into my arms and hugged her tightly. I stepped into the apartment, and she closed the door behind me and locked it. I sat down on the couch, and lowered my head. I guess I was feeling some type of way. I was one of those niggas that didn't mind killing a muhfucka when I had to, but it really wasn't in me to kill senselessly. I felt that was the kind of murders I'd committed the day before.

She sat on the couch on the side of me, picked up my arm, placed it around her shoulders, and laid sideways on my lap.

"What's the matter? And don't tell me nothing because you've never hit me up this late." She flipped on the big screen that I had brought her, and the first thing that popped on was a news report on the massacre that took place in the Mound.

"Princess, turn that shit off," I said, reaching for the remote.

"Why? That's one of the reasons I'm still up. Fourteen people were killed today at one time. Eleven dudesand three females. I been going crazy with worry."

I grabbed the remote from her and turned the TV off. "I don't wanna see no shit like that. That make me think about my little sister."

"I bet, and one of the girls that got killed was just fourteen. Now that's sad. I guess there was a few more that were there and they've been all over Facebook. One of the girls saying something about Jerry Walker. I guess the dudes that got killed must've did something to him."

I shrugged my shoulders. "Yeah, long as you safe, that's all I care about for now. As soon as I saw that shit, I had to make my way over here to make sure that you were good."

She turned on her side and looked me in the eyes. "You fa real?"

I nodded and ran my fingers through her hair. It felt thick, and healthy. "What you been up too?"

She sat all the way up and laid her head on my shoulder. "I been popping this weed at my cousin's house, and for the most part it's been rocking. I went to see Juice yesterday, and all we did was argue. He refuse to tell me who kilt my brother, and I don't know how to take that."

I rubbed her back, and noted that she didn't have a bra on. "Maybe it's in yo best interest that you don't know."

She shot up. "What?"

I took a deep breath, and exhaled. "Calm down. I'm just sayin' if you do find out who did it, how is that going to help you out at all?"

"I'm his sister. I deserve the right to know who killed my brother. And when I find out, I'm gon' kill they ass. And if not me, I got a whole crazy ass Haitian family that will. So I need to know what's good. I know Juice told you, so now I need you to tell me." She got up and knelt down in front of me, looking me directly in the eyes. "Please."

I had to avoid her eye contact because I ain't feel right feeding her a bold face lie. "I don't know who killed him for certain, but I have a few ideas. As soon as I can put a one hundred percent to it, then you'll be the first to know because that is your right." I reached out and stroked her soft cheek. "You understand that."

She took my hand and laid her face into it. "Okay, but just promise me that you'll find out and let me know what's good."

"I promise, when the time is right, you'll know. Now get up here." I pulled her up by her arms and laid her on top of me while I wrapped my arms around her. It was something about the feeling of her small frame against mine. She felt feminine, and she smelled so damn good, just as a woman should.

"Taurus, you never did tell me why you came over here tonight. Is there something wrong?"

I shook my head. "Nall, I just needed somebody to hold while I fell asleep, and who better than you, Princess?"

She slid her hand under my shirt and rubbed my chest while she laid her head on my shoulder. "Ain't nobody better than me. You always tell me that."

"That's right, baby girl." I closed my eyes.

"Taurus?"

"Yeah, Princess."

"Congratulations on the new baby. He's cute, just like his father."

"Thank you, baby girl. Now let's get some sleep before I wind up hittin' that, you rubbin'g all on my thigh."

She giggled. "I didn't even think you peeped that."

"I did. Now let me hold you."

"Okay."

I fell out and didn't awake until about noon the next day. When I woke up, Princess was still in my arms. "Damn, you must've been tired. I done got up at least ten times, and you have not moved from that spot. I know you gotta pee by now."

As soon as she said it, my bladder started to hurt. I mean, I had to piss so bad that I started to pass gas. I hopped up and made my way to the bathroom with her following close behind me.

"I ain't even gon' lie, when you was laying on yo back, yo dick was sticking up so far that I almost did something to you in your sleep. I rubbed myself against that big boy a couple a times."

I wanted to laugh, but if I would have done that, I would have probably pissed on myself. I didn't feel like I could do anything but relieve my bladder. But imagine the feeling I got when I entered into the bathroom just as a nigga was climbing into the window that was above the tub, with a mask on. Before I could even think about it, I rushed him, tackling him into the tub. My bladder released itself and I pissed all in my pants. I didn't even give a fuck. He was a fat strong muhfucka, too.

"Get off me, mane. I come to rob this bitch. This shit ain't got nothin' to do wit you." He struggled against me and almost broke out of my grasp.

"Princess, get the fuck out of here," I yelled.

She ran down the hallway just as this fat muhfucka picked me up and we fell to the bathroom floor with me punching him in the face repeatedly . , I was hitting him hard, with the intent to break his face.

He got to scrambling around like a mad man, bleeding out of his nose and mouth. I had wrestled him into a full Nelsonand I thought I had a perfect hold on him until he slammed his head backward, head butting me in the face. I dropped him immediately. As soon as I did, he went straight for the window and tried to jump out of it, but I had managed to grab his leg.

"Let me go, you son of a bitch!" He hollered, getting ready to kick me in the face.

Princess ran into the bathroom with an angry scowl on her face. I noticed the huge butcher knife in her hand. She raised in over her head and plunged it right into the man's back right between his shoulder blades.

He fell against the window on his chest, then slowly turned around. As soon as he was facing her, she gripped the handle of the knife more firmly with both hands and aimed straight for his chest, once then twice.

"Ahh! Ahhh! Shit!" He uttered as the blade went into him repeatedly.

Blood spurt across Princess's face, as she stabbed him five more times before he slid down into the tub in a pool of his own blood.

"Muthafucka! I don't know what he thought this was," she said, looking down on him in anger.

My chest was rising and falling. I could barely catch my breath. My pants were wet, and I felt like a damn fool having pissed on myself fucking wit that nigga.

She knelt down on the side of me. "Are you okay?"

I looked into her face and saw her for the first time. The fact that she'd just murdered a man meant nothing to her. It was like it didn't phase her at all, and I liked that to the tee. I grabbed her down, and got to kissing all over her lil thick lips. She kissed me back, our tongues dancing to their own beat.

I don't know why the moment had turned me on so much, but we were startled by the arguing in the hallway of her apartment. It sounded like a woman and male were about to go at it. We had to do something wit that body in the tub.

Princess perked up. "Fuck. My neighbors goin' at it again. They always picked the wrong times to do this shit." She left out of the bathroom and closed the door.

Meanwhile, I was stuck in the bathroom with a dead body. I stood up and looked down on the man. His eyes were wide open like he was surprised at what happened to him. I could tell that he was a user because he had track marks all up and down his arms. I took his head and slammed it against the tub again.

"Bitch nigga, what would you've did if I wasn't here?"

I ain't feel no remorse for him at all. In fact, I was sure that I wouldn't even have a bad dream over his ass. Pussy muhfucka preying on a woman. That shit just meant he was a coward.

I could hear Princess talking to the couple in the hallway. She was saying something about it being too early for all of that noise. The next thing I knew, she was in the bathroom with me. "A'ight, what we finna do wit this nigga?" She grabbed a handful of his small afro, and picked his head up.

I looked down at myself. "Don't worry, I'll handle it, but I gotta get some dry clothes first. I'm standing here pissy as a muhfucka."

She nodded in understanding. "There are some jogging pants of mine that are way too big. You can throw them on, or I can wash those for you, and we can wait til they dry. I mean, he ain't going nowhere." She laughed at her own joke.

We wound up going with the latter option while I ran water all over the dead fat man, trying my best to cleanse him of the blood. I took a steak knife, jammed it into his stomach, and pulled it upward, turning him on his stomach so he could bleed down the drain for a few hours.

While I waited for my clothes to dry, I ate me a bowl of cereal. Occasionally, I checked to see how much of the fluids had run out of him.

Princess came back in and handed me my dry clothes. "Here you go. And next time you wanna piss, it's a whole ass toilet right there," she joked.

I nodded my head at her smart ass remark. I found it odd that she could joke while we had a dead man in her tub. "You know you ain't staying here no more, right?"

She nodded. "Yeah, I guess word must be out that I'm here all alone and hustling. I mean, why else would this dude be climbing into my window?" She looked into the tub with anger.

"Well, that shit ain't about to happen no more. After I take care of this punk, we gone put you up in a hotel for the night, and you'll be there until we find you another spot."

She raised her eyebrow. "Why I can't stay wit you? I don't wanna be in some hotel. You got a whole house over there right now." She crossed her arms in front of her chest. "I won't feel safe sleeping nowhere but with you."

That's exactly what wound up happening. I called Tywain,and me and him got rid of the fat dude. We burned his ass up until he was ashes, and then threw the rest of him in the creek. I told him all what happened and he seemed as if he were bored by the whole thing.

"At least Princess got to kill something. I know that shit felt good. Niggaz always get to kill, but when a bitch body something, that shit is special."

That was all he said, and then we moved Princess' things into my mother's old house.

Chapter 10

I changed my son for the first time two days after he was born. I would have done it the first day but I was scared that I was going to hurt him. Shaneeta talked me through the changing process, and I must've looked like a doctor doing brain surgery because I was so careful. He must've thought it was a joke because all he did was smile, and show off his new dimples. Every time I saw them, I felt some type of way.

After I finished changing him, I bounced him around in my arms while Shakia sat on the couch and looked like she was so depressed that she was seconds away from jumping out the window. I didn't pay her no mind because I didn't want her mood to put a damper on how I was feeling for my son. I was happy that he was in the world. In him, I saw a pure version of me.

I Facetimed with my mother while holding him. She complimented him on how handsome he was and promised to spoil him as soon as she saw him. I told her that I would bring him out to Jackson in the next month or so. She was also excited to let me know that she had hired five girls to work in her salon, and that she would be having a grand opening in two weeks.

Shakia got off of the couch and tried to take Tremarion out of my hands. I turned my back to her and held him to my chest.

"Taurus, give him to me. I gotta feed him, my breasts are hurting' me." She reached for him again, and reluctantly I handed him to her. She sat on the couch and pulled down the strap of her gown, exposing a nice supple tittie. It looked so good that I became aroused almost immediately. I felt guilty.

Princess came over, and Shaneeta let her into the house. She walked straight into the living room and right up to me. "How much longer are you going to be over here. I don't want the food getting cold." She looked me in the eyes, and smiled that seductive smile.

"That depends on what you cooked?"

"Yeah, and if it's good enough, I definitely want a plate because a sistah hungry as hell," Shaneeta chimed in, flopping down on the couch.

"Oh, I cooked some ox tails, and a little curry, some greens and cornbread. Just a lil some-some." She looked up to me. "Ain't that what you said you had a taste for?"

I wrapped her into my arms and hugged her, before putting my arm around the small of her back. "Yeah, and I'm about ready to throw down on that."

"Shaneeta, you're more than welcome to come over and eat with us if you want to."

She hopped up off the couch. "Shid, I'mma beat y'all over there." And she must not have been playing because she headed out the front door, and from her windows, I could see her walking across the lawn towards my mother's house.

"Shakia, are you hungry?" Princess asked.

She ignored her at first, until she asked her again. "I'm trying to figure out why you over there living wit my baby daddy. You fuckin' him or something?" She adjusted the baby from one swollen breast to the other. I tried not to look at them because they were doing something to me.

"Look, Taurus, I'mma see you when you get home. I don't feel like arguin' with this girl."

"Bitch, I got yo girl alright," Shakia said, jumping up from the couch. The baby's mouth slipped off of her nipple, and he started to wail at the top of his lungs.

Princess stood there as Shakia ran up into her face. She lowered her head, and curled her top lip. I could tell that she was ready for whatever Shakia wanted to do. She slowly moved her gaze upward until they were locked eye to eye.

"Shakia, now I'm gon' tell you somethin'. If you think you about to put your hands on me and I ain't gon' do nothing about it, you about to be in for a rude awakening. If you touch me in any fashion, I'm gon' handle my business, I can promise you that."

Tremarion continued to cry as Shakia held him on her hip with her right tittie out. "Bitch, don't let me havin' this baby fool you. I get down, too. So if you wanna tear some shit up, we can do that by all means. All I gotta do is give this baby to my baby daddy."

I stood in between them and pushed them apart. "Y'all ain't finna do none of that. Now, Princess, you gone over to the house and I'll be there in a minute. Let me hollaa at Shakia for a second, and y'all don't start eatin' without me."

Princess looked Shakia up and down, and sucked her teeth. "Bitchez think cause I'm small that I don't get down. You betta ask yo baby daddy about how I handle my business before you wind up in a sticky situation." She hugged me. "I'll see you in a minute." She walked out of the door, slamming it shut.

"So you fuckin' that bitch now, too, Taurus?" Shakia questioned, getting all up in my face. "How is it that this bitch is livin' in a house wit you, and me and your son aren't. Explain that shit to me, please." She put his lips back on to her nipple and he stopped crying.

I ran my hands over my face. "Yo, it ain't even like that wit her. Right now, some bullshit happened at her place and she just staying wit me until she get back on her feet. It shouldn't be more than a week."

"A week? How long you think it take for a bitch to get some of yo dick?" She shook her head, and pointed her finger in my face. "You see, that's what's yo problem. You think I'm so fuckin' stupid. You never give me enough credit. I know damn well you fuckin' that bitch. I see how she all over you. You got this bitch in the house cookin' you meals and shit. Meanwhile, me and your son layin' over here unprotected," she scoffed and shook her head. "Damn, I don't get it."

I was so annoyed that I didn't even feel like saying nothing. I hated arguing wit anybody, especially a person I cared about. After she had my son, I didn't even like cussing around her. And when I got irritated, that's all I seemed to do. "Look, Shakia, it ain't that. You always tend to make your assumptions in yo head, and then you get to flippin' out. I ain't got time for that. She gon' be there until she get back on her feet. After that, things will go back to normal."

"Why is she there and we're not? I don't care what your explanation is to why she's there, but why aren't we ?" She stepped closer into my face. "Just give me a clean cut answer and we'll go from there. Don't skate around the answer, don't blow smoke up my ass, just give it to me straight. What gives?"

I moved her out of my personal space a little bit as I began to feel my blood boil.. I didn't know how I was going to react. "Shakia, just cause we got a baby don't mean we finna be together."

" Okay, she livin' there, and y'all not together, so why can't me and your son? *Your* muthafuckin' son! Nigga, explain that to me," she screamed, and tears came running out of her eyes. The baby released her nipple and started to wail with his mouth wide open. "Tell me!"

I tried to grab him out of her arms and she smacked my hands away. "Stop playin' wit me and give me my son. I ain't wit this childish stuff today. Give me my baby until you can get yourself together."

She turned her back on me, and started to walk away. "I'd rather die than to let you get him. You will never get my son again until we livin' under the same roof wit you." She started walking toward the kitchen with him in her arms.

I walked behind her and tapped her shoulder. "Look, Shakia, please don't 'play wit me when it comes to my son. Now I know me and you got things we need to work on, but this baby is precious. We can't allow our differences to affect him in any way."

She turned around and looked me in the eyes. "You don't think by you not being here that it's not affectin' him? It's affectin' me."

"Give me my son, Shakia, I'm not playin' wit you."

"If not, what you gon' do? You gon' hit me. You gon' whoop my ass like your father do your mother? Huh?" She frowned.

"You love this baby more than me already, don't you?"

I could see in her eyes that she was losing her mind. I had to get my son out of her hands. "Give me my son," I said, grabbing him out of her arms. He started screaming , and I turned my back to her, ready to walk out of the kitchen.

She ran to the drawer and opened it, pulling out a steak knife . "Taurus, I swear to God, if you don't give me

my son, I'm gon' kill myself right here in front of you."
Tears dropped from her eyes. "I'm not playin'."

I continued to walk out of the kitchen. "If you do
somethin' that stupid then it's on you. But you not about
to bring that craziness around my son no twenty-four
hours a day."

"Taurus! Please listen to me. If you walk out of that
door with my son, I'm going to end my life. I can't take
what you're doin' to me, anymore. I'm tired of this shit.
I'm too weak. I need you, and the only part of you that I
have is him. So if you take him away from me, if even for
an hour, I will end my life right here tonight."

I turned towards her, preparing to leave out of the
door. "Shakia, I love you, and I always will. But I can't
keep playing these games wit you, ma. Now I've told you
that I'm not ready to settle down wit nobody, and that's
where I still am in my mind. Now for as long as I have
breath in my body you will never have to worry about
nothing. I got you. It may not be in the way you want me
to have you, but as far as you and my son go, y'all will
always be taken care of . Your bills are all mines, and I'm
still gon' pay you child support, and keep you rockin' and
drivin' the latest. I got this ma. Just that, right now, I ain't
ready for no one on one relationship." I took a deep breath.
"I can't see you killin' yourself, but if you do, then that
will be you givin' up on our son, not me. I think you're
way too strong to wimp out like that, though." I turned
around and grabbed the door handle.

"But, Taurus, I need you. I can't do this on my own. I
don't want to live if I can't be your woman. I'm sorry for
sleepin' with your brother. Please forgive me and please
just give me a chance." She dropped down to the floor on
her knees. " Please, you're all we need."

"I would only hurt you, Shakia. I love women too much. I would be less than a man to take you as my woman, knowing that all I'mma do is dog you. So I forgive you for everything that you've done. I also apologize for all of my wrongs. I love you, but I can't be with you. I'll bring our son back in a few hours. Take some time and clear your head."

When I got over to my mother's house, Princess and Shaneeta were in the kitchen getting the food together. I still had Shakia heavy on my heart and I was trying not to dwell on her too much.

Shaneeta took Tremarion out of my hands. "Come mere grandbaby. Let me hold you for minute. Did she give you a bottle for him or anything? "

I shook my head. "Nall, she just needed a minute to breathe. I'm pretty sure she'll be over here in a minute," I said, stepping into the bathroom where I washed my hands.

Princess stepped in behind me and rubbed my back. "Are you okay bro?"

"Yeah, I'm good. I just need to get some food in my system. That girl be driving me crazy. Now we got a son, and its like we gotta get it together."

Princess nodded. "Yeah, I still find it strange that she making this big deal over me and you supposedly messing around when she was fucking Gotto and Juice. I ain't heard about you snapping on her over that."

My heartbeat sped all the way up. I even got a little dizzy. "What you mean she fucked both of them?"

"Oh, you thought she was just fucking Juice or something? Well no, she was screwin' Gotto, too. I actually caught her and Juice getting down twice. That was before me and him decided to become exclusive. By that time, she was already screwin' Gotto, at least that's what Juice said, but I don't know."

I nodded my head hard. All along this bitch had been playing me, her *and* my brothers. There I was thinking that she was this virgin who was giving me the pussy for the first time, when all along, she been fucking them niggas. I got to imagining how Tremarion looked in my mind's eye. He could have been either one of ours. Shit was starting to get really real in my mind.

"I usually don't do the snitchin' thing, but I'm tired of that girl playin' the victim." She rolled her eyes, and continued to rub my back.

"You know what, Princess? I'm glad you told me that. I respect you more than you know for that." I closed the door, and pushed her little ass up against the wall, before lifting her up into the air. She wrapped her legs around me, and I tongued her down, and sucked all over those big juicy lips, at the same time palming her ass. I wanted to hit that pussy right then and there but Shaneeta got to knocking on the door.

"Y'all come on out of there before the food get cold. You can only heat it up so many times before it don't taste right. Now let's go."

I put her down, and she stood on her tippy toes and kissed me hard with her arms wrapped around the back of my neck.

"I want you tonight, the way I'm supposed to have you. Do you get that?"

I most definitely did.

When we got into the living room, Shaneeta had the table laid out with the food. Our plates were already made and I didn't waste no time going in. The food was delicious.

"So how long y'all been fucking?" Shaneeta asked, at the same time sipping out of her glass of Fruit Punch.

Princess dropped her fork. "What is with you and your daughter? Why are y'all steady trying to put us in the bed together?"

"Because when I just put my ear to the bathroom door, it sounded like y'all was mouth fucking. So if you doin' that when you got company over, what do you do when ain't nobody here?" She bit into her chicken. "So how long y'all been fuckin'?"

"We ain't fucked yet, but when you leave tonight, it's gon' be the first time because I gotta have me some of him," Princess said, and then sucked her bottom lip. "Is that blunt enough for you?"

Shaneeta shrugged her shoulders and closed her eyes. "As long as you save me some, I don't care one way or the other. His dick big enough to go around."

All I could do was shake my head. I was listening to them, but at the same time I was thinking about what Princess had told me. "Shaneeta, on some real shit, did you know that Juice and Gotto was both fucking your daughter?"

She nodded. "Yeah, and?"

"And, what are the odds that Tremarion is really my son?"

She shrugged her shoulders, and sat back in her chair. "To be honest with you, I don't know. My daughter made a lot of wrong decisions, and it's not my place to say what is what. "

"Is there any chance that Tremarion is not my son?"

She lowered her head, and exhaled loudly. "He's definitely your blood. But as far as your son goes, there's a thirty-three point three percent chance that he is. But the same percentage goes to both of your brothers."

As she said that, Shakia stepped into the living room. The first thing I noted was that she had slit both of her wrists so deep that blood was spurting out of them. "Why did you tell him that, momma? That was not yo business to tell." She took the knife and stabbed herself in the chest with it, and fell to her knees, and then her face.

Shaneeta ran to her side. "Oh my God, Shakia, what did you do? What have you done, baby?" She tried to grab her and force her onto her lap. "Somebody call the ambulance. Please, somebody call the ambulance."

Princess looked at me with a smirk on her face. Then she kept on eating her food. She even had the nerve to burp once.

I sat at the table for about two extra minutes before I picked Shakia up and took her back over to their house, and laid her on the living room floor. By this time Shaneeta had already called the ambulance.

We buried her six days later at Pleasant View Cemetery. It was all surreal to me, at first. I didn't really know how to feel, or what to think, so I tried not to do either one. The bottom line was that Tremarion's mother was dead. Whether she meant anything to me or not, that was still his mother, but I still didn't know how to feel.

Princess stood in front of me, and I wrapped my arms around her. She leaned her head back into my chest as we overlooked Shakia's grave. Everybody else had left, yet we'd stayed behind to pay our last respects.

"You okay up there?" she asked in her small voice.

"I mean, it is what it is. Now I gotta get a DNA test to see if he's mine. Either way, I'mma make sure him and Shaneeta straight for life."

"That's what's up." She looked into the grave. "Damn, that girl had some issues, though."

"Yeah."

I saw Tywain's truck rolling though the graveyard at full speed. I mean, he even knocked down a few headstones. He slammed on the brakes, and jumped out of his truck. "Yo, that fool Serge done snapped out, bro. He just snatched up your son, and my daughter."

"Wait, what are you talking about? I thought Cassie was still pregnant?"

He lowered his head. "She was eight months. That fool Serge cut the baby out of her, and slit her throat. He threw my baby moms over the bridge at Chesapeake. I found her hanging from a rope over the water."

"What the fuck he snappin' out about?" I asked, thinking that I had just seen Tremarion less than an hour ago with his grandmother. I started to think about my mother and sister.

Tywain looked down to Princess, and then up to me. He wrapped his arm around my neck and walked me away from her. The clouds got darker over our heads. I could smell the rain beginning to form in them.

"Dang, so y'all gone keep secrets and shit. If y'all in danger, don't you think that I am too." She ran over to where we were and blocked our path. "Taurus, when me and you start keeping secrets?"

Tywain slid his arm from around my neck.

"Princess I don't think you need to be involved in this shit. We dealing wit a psycho ass dude that got a cold heart, especially for our people. Now the less you know, the better." I started to walk off with Tywain again.

She walked in front of us. "I don't care if it's dangerous, if it got anything to do wit you, then it's my business. I care about you, too, Tywain. I'll die beside both of you niggas wit no hesitation." She looked from him and back to me. " So tell me what's good?"

Tywain looked down to me and I shrugged my shoulders.

"Bro, whatever you finna tell me, she can hear, too. I think she earned that right."

Tywain raised his eyebrow. "Nigga, you sho'?"

I nodded my head. "One hunnit percent. Tell me?" Tywain shrugged his shoulders. "I don't give a fuck about that nigga anyway. Look, when Juice and Pac Man kidnapped Serge's daughter and son, what they didn't know was that he had cameras all in that farm house. For some reason, them niggas exposed their self when they went in there, and Serge got both of their faces on camera. Not only that, but Juice's phone number was in his son's cell."

"Wait, so you're saying that the white boy that was found next to my brother was this guy's son? So if he was killed at the same time as my brother, then why was Juice able to walk away from everything unscathed? Then, on top of that, what does it have to do with you two?"

"Serge asked us a bunch of times if we knew what took place with this whole thing, and we told him that we didn't. I'm thinking that he might be feeling like we had something to do with it and we made a fool of him and his family. But since he can't really prove it, he hollering this eye for an eye shit."

"That's why he took your daughter, because his daughter got took, and that's why he took my son, because his son was taken."

"No, Taurus, his son wasn't just taken, he was murdered," Princess said barely above a whisper.

That sent chills all the way down my spine. I had missed that fact, and I shouldn't have. "So you think this nigga about to kill my son?"

Tywain lowered his head. "Knowing how he get down, probably bro."

I didn't know how to take that. I mean, yeah, I didn't even know if Tremarion was my kid or not, but at the same time it was just like Shaneeta had said, no matter what, he was my blood, and he was just a baby. It was my job to protect him because my name was on that birth certificate.

Tywain fell to the ground on his knees. "Yo, I been wanting a daughter for forever, man. I can't believe he did Cassie like that. She was a good girl. She ain't deserve that shit."

I knelt down and rubbed his back. I wasn't feeling all that emotional over my situation with Tremarion like that because I didn't know if he was my kid or not. I mean, I felt vengeful, and like I wanted to get even with the Russian. But I didn't feel like I was losing a child. I knew that was crazy, but the whole Shakia fooling me and low key fucking both of my brothers thing was still eating at me.

"Yo, what you wanna do kid?"

Princess was pacing back and forth with her head down. The rain started to pour from the sky, and it didn't seem to bother her one bit. She had her hands bent so that they rested on her lower back. She looked to be in deep thought. I even saw her lips moving as if she were talking to herself.

Tywain stood up with the rain beating off of his face. "He wanna have a sit down. My grandfather says that we need to face him like men. He said that if we ain't got shit to hide then we would face him, and get our children back.

We're suppose to meet him tonight at 9 pm at the butcher's warehouse."

"What? That could be a trap, bro. What if he wanna meet wit us just so he can fuck us over like we supposedly did his kids? Something don't seem right about that spot."

Tywain swung at the air five times, and then fell back to his knees. "I don't give a fuck. I'm going to get my daughter. I'm not gone let this punk ass Russian treat me like no pussy. Now we ain't have shit to do wit what Juice nem' did. He supposed to be going at him, not at no innocent children that ain't even really have a chance to come into this world. I'll be there. I just hope you on side of me."

Chapter 11

As soon as we pulled up to the warehouse, Serge's men surrounded my truck with assault rifles that had beams on the tops of them. I had so many red lights pointed at my forehead that I was afraid to move from fear that some trigger happy Russian would blow my brains out.

They beat on my driver side window and did the same to the passenger's. I was glad that I had put Princess up in a hotel. All of this would have surely freaked her out. She already seemed as if she were not herself since hearing the news that involved her brother.

As they beat on the window, they ordered for me to pop the locks on the door. I looked over at Tywain and he had a smug look on his face that said he wasn't impressed. "Whatever we do, bro, we do it together."

"No doubt, kid. Let's roll."

I popped the locks, and they ripped us from the truck, and threw us to the ground. I felt a knee on the back of my neck, and then handcuffs being fastened around my wrists. I could hear handcuffs fastening in the distance and I figured that everything they were doing to me, they were doing to Tywain also.

A black pillowcase like thing was put over my head, and I couldn't see anything but pure darkness as they led us inside of the warehouse. I mean, they handled me rough, too. More than once somebody punched me in the stomach. And another person would kick me in the ass. Dead in the center, too, that shit hurt worse than the stomach punches.

Finally, we made it to our destination, and I was made to sit in an uncomfortable chair that felt like steel. When the pillowcase was taken off of my head, I saw that we were in something like a cooler. Big slabs of meats hung around our heads on hooks. They looked like the bodies of cows that had been stripped of their skin. We were seated at a big round metal table. There were about twenty of Serge's Russian men surrounding us with scowls on their faces. They gave us looks that said they couldn't wait to kill us.

I looked over to Tywain, and he still didn't look impressed. He looked like whatever they were getting ready to do, he was prepared for. I tried to gain some courage from his demeanor.

I was personally ready for whatever they had in mind, but I didn't really know if I was prepared for death that night. The main people I kept thinking about was my mother and sister. I prayed that they were safe and sound.

Serge came in, with Russell close behind him. He had on a plastic apron, and in his hand was a meat hook. He came to the table and slammed it down so loud that it pissed me off.

"So you two chose to come and see me. I am surprised that you had such balls."

Tywain straightened up in his seat. "Where the fuck is my daughter? Yo, you ain't have to kill her moms like that, Serge. We ain't have shit to do with your kids being snatched up."

Russell stepped up and smacked Tywain so hard that he fell backward out of his seat. "You watch the way you talk to him, lil nigga. I don't give a fuck if you're my grandbaby or not, I'll murder you right here and right now."

Serge pointed to his fallen chair, and one of his henchmen picked Tywain back up and fixed his chair so that he sat upright.

"You have done enough lying to me, Tywain. I don't trust a word that comes out of your mouth anymore. You or that one sitting next to you," he said, pointing at me. "Now one of you are going to tell me what I want to know, or I am going to torture you in the worst way before killing you."

I adjusted myself in my chair. I felt like making a run for it. We should have known that he was finna be on some torture shit. I mean, why else would he have us meet him in a meat warehouse?

Serge walked over to me and grabbed me by the neck. "You scum bag, tell me what happened to my kids. Where is Nastia, and is she dead like my son?" He spat in my face.

I wanted to rush his ass. The worst thing a person could ever do to you while they were hollering at you was spit in your face. It didn't matter if it was on purpose or accident. Both of them were equally gross and disrespectful to me.

"Do you hear me, fucker? Where is my daughter? And what happened to my son?"

I didn't even know that Nastia was missing in action because I had been so wrapped in Shakia's dilemma. Now that he said it, I started to panic, not only because she was missing, but because she would have been the only one to save us from this predicament. "I don't know what you talking about, Serge. I haven't heard from her in a few weeks."

Serge snapped his fingers over his head, and backed away from the table. "So this is the game that you want to play, huh? Okay, it works for me."

I looked up and a big beefy henchman came through the doors of the huge cooler with Shaneeta. She had duct tape around her mouth and he was leading her forward by grasping a handful of her hair. Her eyes were closed, and her face looked like he was hurting her the way she kept on wincing, and squeezing them tightly. The man slammed her face and mid-section on the table, and put his elbow into the back of her neck.

Serge walked over to her and grabbed a handful of her hair, picking her head up off of the table. "Since you don't want to tell me what I need to know, I'm going to show you how we do it back where I am from. Grab her hand," he ordered Russell.

Russell grabbed her hand, and put it into the middle of the table. Shaneeta tried to ball it into a fist, but he smashed her hand with his elbow. "Open yo hand, bitch, and take this like a woman." He struggled for a second and then he finally got her hand to lay flat on the table.

Serge looked me straight in the eye before one of his henchmen handed him a meat cleaver. "So for every minute that you waste without telling me the truth, I am going to cut off one of her fingers. I know that you care about this woman, Taurus. I know that you don't want me to do this. All I want to know is what happened to my kids. It's the only thing that matters to me." He tied the sash to his apron tighter. "Russell, hold her steady." He ripped the duct tape away from her mouth.

"You have one last chance, Taurus. Tell me what I need to know. Who killed my son? And where is my daughter?"

"Please, Taurus, baby. Don't let them do this to me. Please tell him what he needs to know."

Serge smiled, "You should listen to her, Taurus. I'm pretty sure she needs her fingers for something."

"Probably to flip him the bird after all this," Russell said, cracking a weak ass joke and laughing his ass off.

"Tell me what you're gonna do, guys." He looked from me to Tywain.

I lowered my head because I didn't know what to tell him. I mean, anything that I said wasn't gone be the right thing. I hated to see Shaneeta in that position, especially after she'd just lost her daughter, and had gotten shot in the back because of Juice. I felt like she was paying the consequences for shit that she didn't have nothing to do with.

"Yo, Serge, let her go, man. Your beef ain't with this innocent woman, it's with me and Tywain. If you gone torture somebody, you can take your anger out on me first. Just let her go because she don't know nothing about nothing."

Serge laughed at the top of his lungs. "Oh, I fully intend on taking my anger out on you very shortly, but for now, I want to have some fun. So are you telling me what I need to know, or not?" He looked down at me, and I lowered my head. "What about you, Tywain? No, nothing? Okay then."

He raised the cleaver over his head and brought it down so fast and hard that it chopped Shaneeta's thumb right off from her hand. The thumb shot off the top of the metal table and landed on the floor by my foot, it still had the ring on it.

At first, her eyes got really big. Then she looked down, and the next thing I knew, she was screaming at the top of her lungs as if somebody was killing her. The blood kept on spurting from her thumb hole.

I turned my head away, and when I looked back, she was throwing up all over the table. I damn near wanted to puke myself. I looked over to Tywain and all he did was curl his top lip.

"Now tell me what happened to my son. Why did your brother rob my children? And how did they all know each other? Where is my daughter now?"

I sat all the way up in my seat while Shaneeta cried, looking at me like I had failed to protect her. She looked sick, and that broke my heart. Had there been anything that I could have done to protect her, I would have. I felt like a bitch just sitting there while everything took place.

"Yo, that shit foul as hell. We ain't have no business with your children at all. From as far as I know, your son was doing heroin with his brother. He must've got to running his mouth too much and told Juice about the safe house. And Juice being the dope fiend that he is, he robbed him. How your son got murdered along with the order dude is beyond me. But we ain't have shit to do with it," Tywain ranted.

Serge raised the meat cleaver and slammed it down, taking off Shaneeta's forefinger. This time he chopped it off with so much force that it bounced off of the table and into my lap. He raised it again, and chopped off her middle finger as well.

She screamed at the top of her lungs, and then passed out on top of the table. Serge turned the cleaver to the side and smacked her so hard that she woke up crying.

"Please. Please, stop this. I can't take no more. You chopping off my fucking fingers!"

I tried to get up but two of the guards came over and slammed me back into my chair. "That's bullshit. He picking on a female. What type of bitch shit is that?"

One of his henchmen punched me in the jaw, snapping my neck backward. I saw blue lightning, and then he backhanded me.

"Permission to waste this pig, boss?"

"Tell me what I want to know!" Serge took the cleaver and chopped off the last two of Shaneeta's fingers on her right hand. It was a bloody mess on the table. He picked up her pinky finger and put it into his mouth, chewing on it.

Russell took her other hand and placed in on the table in the same fashion that he'd done the last one. "I sho' hope y'all tell him what he need to know before she run out of digits. That's gone be so sad," he joked, laughing so hard he had to take a deep breath just to continue.

"Yo, Serge, chill, man. My brother and your son did dope together, just like Tywain said. He didn't even kill your son, the other nigga that was found wit him did. That's why he killed him, because that wasn't a part of the game plan. From what I was told, they were just supposed to rob the house and leave, but my brother's accomplice had other ideas in mind. He thought that there was more money and product somewhere else and that your son was lying about them having found it all. To send a message to your daughter, he killed him in front of her in the hopes that she would give up the rest of the information in regards to the rest of everything."

"And how do you know this? Most importantly, why didn't you tell me this from the get go?"

"That shit ain't have nothing to do with me. That was my brother's fuck up. My job was to make sure that he didn't hurt Nastia, and I did that. I got there too late to save your son. But I did save your daughter, and that gotta count for something."

Serge smiled sinisterly. He raised the cleaver and chopped off the rest of Shaneeta's fingers. He then grabbed her by the hair and threw her into the arms of Russell. "Get rid of her. And bring me the baby." He wiped his mouth with the bloody cleaver in his hand.

Me and Tywain perked up. I think we were both wondering which baby he was talking about. Was it Tywain's daughter, or was it my son? Our answer came moments later when Russell came in carrying Tremarion in his arms. He bounced him up and down and held a bottle in his mouth.

Serge took the baby from Russell and placed him in the center of the table. "Now things are going to get a lot more interesting." He looked at me and smiled. "Tell me why I should not believe that you were a part of this whole thing? Why should I not go with my gut?"

I looked at him for a long time with my face frowned. I was tired of submitting to his bitch ass. I hated his pink face. I hated the way Russell followed behind him like a little lap dog. And I didn't like how he'd just treated Shaneeta. I didn't know if she was dead or alive.

"We ain't have shit to do with that. Our only dealings was finding your daughter and bringing her home safe to you. That's it, and for that you should be grateful." Tywain spit on the floor.

"Grateful, huh? Far as I'm concerned, you killed my son, and now I'll kill yours." He raised the cleaver up in the air, and I turned my head away before he could bring it down in time. I felt warm fluid coat my face, and the baby screaming. Then I heard the sound of the blade coming down again and again and hitting cushion. Every time it came down more fluid splashed my face until it pooled into my mouth. It tasted like a copper penny. I felt sick to my stomach. I refused to look at what had taken place. It took me five full minutes to open my eyes. When I did, I saw Russell smearing the table off into a black plastic bag. I heard something drop into the bag again and again, but I couldn't have been for sure as to what it was. But I had an idea. The table's top was drenched in blood. It was so bad that it dripped off the edges of the table.

"Now that I've taken your son. There is still the matter of my daughter. Where is she?" Serge asked, kneeling down into my face.

I didn't say a word. I almost spit in his face. I was so mad that I felt my vision going blurry. I was shaking, and I knew that one day I would kill the Russian. I didn't know how I felt emotionally about him killing Tremarion. I think, at that moment, it was so fresh that it didn't affect me the way that it was supposed to. I wasn't sad. I wasn't sick over it. I just felt like I had to get revenge for a family member's death. I didn't feel like he had killed my son, and I think it was because of the revelations of Shaneeta. I feared more for Tywain's daughter.

"Serge, we ain't got her, man. There would be no reason for us to have your daughter. Just think about it. What the fuck would we gain by kidnapping her?"

Serge stood up shaking his head. "I don't know, but we'll find out soon enough." He snapped his fingers, and Russell stepped back into the room wheeling an incubator. When he got all the way into the room, I was able to see a little baby wrapped in a pink blanket inside. She had IVs in her tiny arms, and small oxygen tubes up her nose.

"Now this is going to be a little harder for me." He looked at the ceiling as if he were trying to stop himself from crying. He even fanned his eyes.

"You see, this is my best friend's granddaughter, and the last thing I want to do is to kill his grandbaby. So what I am thinking is this. I've already gotten even by taking the life of your son, because your brother took the life of mine. Whether he pulled the trigger or not, he was part of it all. Therefore, you had to pay for his sins since he don't have any children." He shrugged his shoulders. "That's just the way it goes, buddy. Now you two did bring my daughter Nastia back to me alive. So I am going to give you a chance. I won't kill this girl child just yet. I'll give you one week to bring my daughter home to me alive. And if you can do that, I will hand this child over to you. However, if you do not, I will have no other choice than to dispose of her, just like I did the other one. My daughter is my everything and I have a feeling that if I killed the both of you right now, I would never find her. So I am giving you a chance to return her to me alive and I will do the same for this child. You have one week. If you fail me, things will get very ugly for the both of you."

Chapter 12

"Bitch nigga got my daughter. Muhfucka done kilt my baby momma, and hung her over a bridge. He kilt yo son and Shaneeta. Man, I could kill that nigga Juice, man. We always gotta clean up this nigga mess. Then what is he doing? Shit. That fuck nigga laying back in his bunk without a care in the world. He don't give a fuck about you. He don't give a fuck about me. That nigga wouldn't care if we told him everything that's going on. He'd probably just shrug his shoulders and go back to doing whatever he was doing," Tywain said, pacing back and forth in front of my truck as we were parked at the lake front.

Princess walked up to me and laid her head on my chest. "Dang, he killed yo son? I'm sorry to hear that, Taurus." She reached up and pulled my forehead down so that it touched hers.

"So what are we gonna do?"

Tywain grabbed his bottle of Hennessy and chugged it. "I don't know, but I ain't finna let this nigga kill my daughter. I ain't even held her in my arms yet. My punk ass grandfather got to do that before I did. Fuck." He threw the bottle down on the ground, and squeezed his head in both of his hands. "This shit driving me crazy."

The alcohol had spilled all over my pants, but I didn't even give a fuck. I was so shell shocked that I didn't know what to do. "Bro, you just gotta keep calm. You know we'll figure this shit out. We always do."

"Yo, I could kill that nigga Juice." He punched at the air, and spun around on the balls of his feet. "Yo, Princess, you know that nigga killed your brother right?"

"Bro!"

"Nall, fuck that," he said, waving me off. "That bitch nigga killed yo brother and buried him just like he buried that white dude. That nigga grimey. He don't give a fuck about you, me, or nobody else."

Princess broke out of my embrace and looked me in the eye. "Is it true, Taurus. Did he really kill my brother?"

At that time, I was so irritated and tired of covering for Juice that I just didn't care no more. "Yeah, he killed him. I ain't know how to tell you. That's the only reason I didn't. Juice said that he was gone tell you in his own time. After he heard that me and you were in contact out here, he thought that I was just gone tell you what he did. So he called me out to the prison and told me not to tell you. He said that he would tell you in his own time, and at the right time. Every day I was waiting for him to, but I guess he didn't," I said, even though I knew most of it was false. I just didn't need to fall out with her. I was starting to care about her a lot, and I didn't want us to fallout over something that Juice did.

She blinked tears into her eyes. "Damn, and here I was trusting you with all of me," she said so low that I could barely hear her.

Tywain pulled her into his embrace. "Nall, fuck that, Princess. Don't get salty at my mans because it ain't his fault. It's that nigga Juice's. He got everybody paying for his sins. That shit foul as hell. Here he was fucking wit you like you was his woman, and all along he bodied your brother. That's fuck nigga shit. I should've been bodied his ass. He lucky he was yo brother, Taurus. Word is bond."

Princess shook her head and wiped her tears away. "I guess a part of me knew he had something to do wit it. I just didn't know to what extent. But now I do. So what are we going to do about this white girl?"

I shrugged my shoulders. "I guess we gotta find her. I mean, what other choice do we have?" I walked over to Princess and grabbed her to my chest. "Me and you gon' talk about this shit. Don't think I'm not gon' give you an explanation, because I am. I respect you more than that. But you gotta understand what kind of position I was in."

"I do," she said, looking at the ground. "It's not yo fault. Juice just played me. I wonder what his end game was."

"That nigga too stupid to have one," Tywain said, frowning.

***

Nastia hit me up on Facebook at three in the morning, and told me to meet her at Boogaloos. I was in the bed hugged up with Princess, unable to fall asleep. Me and her had had a long talk that night. I explained to her where I was coming from, and why I didn't tell her right away. It took a long time to get her to calm down. The only thing she kept on saying was that she looked up to me more than that, and that I could have been kept shit real with her and allowed her to process things for herself. She said she didn't like thinking that I was just like every other man that had stepped foot in her life. All those that only lied to her and told her what she wanted to hear. I promised that from then on I would always keep shit one hunnit wit her, no matter what. After our long talk, we got into the bed and she asked me to hold her all night, which I had no problem doing.

When Nastia hit me up, I damn near jumped out of the bed. I wanted to call Tywain right away, but she told me not to contact anybody else, so I didn't. I felt bad about not getting at the homey right away, but I felt it was in our best interest for me to follow her directives. So I let her know that I would be there in a an hour.

I tried to get out of the, bed but Princess had her legs and arms wrapped all over my body. Every time I moved she acted as if she wanted to wake up. Finally, after trying for ten minutes to not wake her up, I just got irritated and nudged her.

Her eyes popped open. "Huh? What? What's going on?" she asked, sitting up.

I kissed her on the forehead. "Chill, ma, you good. Look, I gotta make a run. I should be back in a few hours."

Now she was wide awake. "You ain't about to go nowhere without me. You betta wait until I get dressed." She jumped out of the bed clad only in her tight pink Victoria Secret boy short panties that hugged her ass so right. I damn near tackled her. She didn't have no bra on, and her small titties bounced on her chest. Even though I was feeling some type of way about life, her body sparked something in me.

I grabbed her and pulled her to me, leaning down and sucking all over her juicy lips. Her tongue attacked mine, and she started to breathe harder into my mouth. I was breathing just as hard as I squeezed that ass and sucked on her neck.

When my dick got hard, I pressed it into her stomach, and she moaned. I was ready to snatch her lil ass up but I had to remember the task at hand, so I pulled her up off her knees when she sank to them and pulled my dick out.

"Yo, we gone handle this later. For now, I gotta go handle this business. I'll be back in a minute."

"No, I don't want you to leave me in this house with all this bullshit going on. Please take me wit you."

"Princess, listen to me. This the white girl that they been looking for. If I can return her to her father, all this shit can be over and done with, and we can get the fuck out of Memphis without going to war with all of Russia. Now you gotta trust me on this."

She stroked my piece up and down. Leaned her head down and sucked him into her mouth. As soon as I felt her hot lips wrap around him, I stood up on my tippy toes and closed my eyes. Her mouth felt so good that I could barely take it. It had been a little while since I'd gotten some ass, and even if my brain knew I wasn't supposed to be focused on no shit like that, my dick didn't. She bobbed her head up and down him so fast that I was on the verge of coming before I got the chance to really enjoy it. When I felt her tongue running up and down my penis slit. I came all in her mouth, and she kept on stroking me for dear life until I was done.

Afterwards, she kissed me on the lips. "Okay, baby, you go do what you gotta do. But then you get back here and you handle yo business wit me." She took my hand, pulled her panties to the side, and ran my fingers up and down her juicy slit. I slid two fingers in her and felt her warmth and tightness. I was duly impressed.

"You get my drift."

When I pulled up into Boogaloo's parking lot, Nastia was nowhere to be found. I went on to Facebook to see if she was on there or not. When I confirmed that she wasn't, I sent her a text, and told her that I was there waiting. Fifteen minutes later, somebody on a motorcycle pulled into the parking lot, wearing all black, with a black helmet and everything. When they pulled on the side of my truck,

I put my Tech .9 on my lap and cocked it at the top. I was ready to wet some shit. There was no way that I was gone allow nobody to just body me without eating a buffet of bullets.

Nastia pulled off the helmet and waved me out of the truck.

I got out of my truck, and walked over to her. "Get on the back, and hurry up. I think I'm being followed."

"If you think you being followed, why the fuck would you lead them to my truck?" I asked, looking around and not seeing nothing or nobody. I didn't know the first thing to riding on a Ducatti, and I was feeling some type of way that it was looking like I was going to have to.

"Taurus, I don't have time to argue with you right now. Just get on the freaking bike and screw that truck. I'll buy you another one. Let's go!"

I reached into my truck and grabbed my tech, and jumped on the back of her bike. As soon as I sat down, she gunned the engine, and we took off at full speed. I damn near fell off the back of it. I wrapped my arms around her waist and held her tight as hell.

As we were rolling down the street that Boogaloo's was on, there were three black Suburban trucks coming our way on the other side of the street. As soon as we rode past them, they slammed on their brakes. I looked back to see them hitting U-turns before storming behind us at rapid speeds.

Nastia gunned her bike, and it took off. She drove onto the sidewalk when we came to an intersection, and the light turned red. She made a right on the side walk, and the bike still wound up going into the street and nearly slamming into a white pickup truck that had a washing machine in back of it. We missed it by a few feet.

As soon as that moment passed. She stormed away and we got on to the highway going ninety miles an hour. I looked over my shoulder to see the Surburbans not that far behind. They were picking up speed, and I was worried when I saw a man hanging out of the window with an AK in his hand. Seconds later, the same man got to shooting at us with rapid fire. Nastia maneuvered the bike so that it went from side to side.

I was so worried about getting hit in the back that I aimed the Tech, and squeezed the trigger at the truck that was firing at us. The bullets sprayed across the window, and the driver swerved into the other lane and crashed into a semi-truck that carried it for all of a hundred yards. One of the other Suburbans sped up, and another man got to shooting at us from out of the passenger's window.

Nastia gassed the bike a little more and got to weaving in and out of cars. The shooter kept on shooting from his assault rifle. His bullets shattered the back of one car's windows. And as he shot some more, I noted the car's windshield turn red. Then the car crashed into another car that was driving in the lane on side of it before flipping over three times and exploding. The Suburban crashed right into the mayhem, and carried the other car into another one, before that one flipped over as well.

Nastia kept on gunning the bike until she eventually hit an exit and we wound up on a dirt road with the other Suburban still following close behind. She stormed on to the dirt path, and made a right into some woods. I didn't know where she was going and I was starting to feel real uneasy. When we drove about three yards and the bike slowed down as if she were getting ready to stop. I really started to lose my mind. And then she cut the engine off, and we fell off the bike on to our sides.

She took off her helmet. "Come on, follow me."

She took off running, with me following behind her. We were running through tall grass that was still wet from the storm that had passed over earlier that night. It was so dark that I was worried about running into a tree, or falling into a swamp somewhere. But she kept on running, and I tried my best to stay as close to her as possible.

The wet grass slapped against my legs, and made them itch. I could hear Crickets all around us, and the only light we could see was that of the moon. She ran to a tunnel that led into the small lake, and pulled me inside. "Listen, Taurus, these men are trying to kill me. They think that I am going to expose their secrets about the elections down here in the States, but I have no intentions on doing that." She pulled me down so that I was crouching on one knee. "You have to get rid of them for me, please."

My heart was beating so fast that I didn't know what to do. I could barely breathe. My legs were itching worse than I could ever remember. It felt like a bunch of little bugs were crawling all over me, and even biting me off and on.

"Nastia, what the fuck is going on? Yo father think that me and Tywain kilt you. He bodied my son, and threatened to kill Tywain daughter if we don't find you." I could hear the trampling of grass in the distance. That let me know that the men were trying to find us. Looking out into the woods that we had come from, I could also see flashlights.

Nastia grabbed my shirt. "Listen to me, Taurus. I am involved in some shit way deeper than you know. I helped the KGB put your president into the White House. And it's not the KGB that you're familiar with. I'm talking about an Underworld Government Mafia that is dead set on starting a New World Order. They are looking to make it a one world currency. They would be in charge of all of the finances throughout the whole world. This would make them more powerful than our vision of God on this Earth. Russia wants to lead this Regime, and the only way for them to be leaders is if they took out the most powerful country on earth, which is the United States. They had to put somebody into the White House that would follow all of their directives. Well that man has been elected. And since he's been in office they've been getting flack from the CIA. They've been given the order to kill everybody that had anything to do with the rigging of the election. I was one of them. I helped to get him elected by using my cyber skills, and connections. Now they want me dead. "

I heard the trampling getting closer. I didn't know what the fuck she was talking about, but I knew I had to get away from her because she was involved in something serious. I was trying to figure out how I could get her back to her father, so that we cleared our names, but at the same time break away from her.

"Look, Nastia, I'll do whatever you want me to do. Just tell me what to do."

Her eyes got as big as saucers, and then she upped two .45 automatics. She pushed me with all of her might. "Taurus, watch out," she screamed, and fired four loud shots over my head.

Boom! Boom! Boom! Boom!

I heard somebody holler out and then they fell on top of me. I pushed the body off of me and raised my weapon, but by that time, Nastia had run out of the tunnel and I could hear her firing again. I ran behind her as shots were fired in our direction. In the dark of the night, it was the only light that we could see besides the moon. I crouched down on the side of her. "Who the fuck is you, girl?"

"Taurus, there is so much that you don't 'know about me. But one thing I want you to know is that I really love you. And when this is all over, you and I are going to vacation together somewhere."

I saw one somebody running toward us with an assault rifle in his hand. When he saw Nastia, he bent down to aim his weapon, and that's when I put about ten shots in his face. The bullets chopped through the meat of his face, and split it apart. I grabbed Nastia up by her arm and we ran back into the woods, until we came to a small swamp. That was where I was ready to draw the line because when I looked into it all I could see was six pairs of red eyes, and that meant there were alligators.

"Taurus, listen to me. I have a motor boat on the other side. If we can just get to it, we can get out of here and I can take you to my father and you can squash things with him. There is no other way. I'm pretty sure those men have called back up by now. I don't want them knowing who you are. If they find out who you are, your entire family will suffer tremendously. Trust me on this." She grabbed my hand.

I yanked it away. "You gotta be out of yo mind. It's alligators in there. You think they gon' hesitate to eat our ass up?" I shook my head so hard that I got a headache. I heard a Helicopter overhead, and it had a big searchlight casting over the woods.

"You see what I'm telling you. We have to go, now." She pulled my hand, and I followed her into the water.

I felt like I was going to get bit in any minute. I felt hysterical and ready to lose my mind, especially when one pair of red eyes turned toward us, and then dropped underwater. I started to swim faster than I evr thought I could. I felt the cold water going all into my mouth and ears. It was thick with seaweeds, and all kinds of other stuff. When another pair of red eyes dropped into the water, I thought I was going to faint, especially when I felt something rough nudge my waist. I mean it bumped me real hard, so hard that it threw off my swimming motion.

Nastia was way up ahead of me, damn near on to land already and I was just in the middle of the creek. I had never been any good at swimming, and that was the wrong time to not be. When something bumped me on my other side, I damn near shit on myself. I said fuck that. I got to squeezing the trigger on my weapon, and pointing it all underwater and in the direction of the red eyes. I didn't care if I hit them or not, I was trying to make it out of that water alive.

When I felt sharp teeth start to bite down on my side, I pressed my gun right to the beast's head and pulled the trigger. The animal vibrated for a minute, and then floated up in the water in front of me on its back. I pushed it out of the way and swam to land.

Chapter 13

"Dad, you need to let this go. They saved me from losing my life, and Taurus just did it again. We have bigger fish to fry." She squeezed tears out of her eyes. "Our government wants me dead because I carried out a mission that you gave me. They tried to kill me tonight. And if Taurus had not been there, I would have been a goner."

Serge slammed his hand down on the table. "That fucking Sessions! He and Flynn assured me that a hair would not be touched on your head. This means war!" He turned to Russell and snapped his fingers.

Russell left, and when he came back into the room, I damn near threw up. Not only was he holding Tywain's daughter in his arms, but he had my mother and Mary on the side of him.

Both of their mouths were covered with duct tape, and their hands were bound.

"Taurus, as I said before, things were going to take a turn for the worst." He looked to my sister and mother. "Thank you for saving my daughter, once again. This officially makes us even because you have given me an eye for the eye that your brother took." He twirled his finger in the air and Russell cut my mother and sister lose, taking the duct tape from their mouths.

They ran to me and wrapped their arms around me. "Baby, I thought these men were gonna kill us," my mother said, holding me tight and crying hard.

"Yeah, they took me out of my bedroom and smacked me a bunch of times." I could see that my sister's face was red on one side, just as was my mother's.

"That's okay, just as long as y'all are alive. I would never let nothing happen to my babies."

Russell handed Tywain his daughter. Tywain fell to his knees holding her. She was wrapped in a pink blanket, and even though she had her eyes closed in a deep sleep, I could tell that she looked just like the homey.

"Tywain, I'm sorry that you got caught in the middle of this, but you only suffered a minor casualty. I do apologize, but we have to move forward."

Nastia walked over to me and hugged me tightly. "Taurus, when I get things in order, I'm coming for you. I need you because there is something I need to tell you when the time is right." She whispered the last part in my ear, kissed me on the cheek, and walked away to stand by her father's side.

I put my mother and sister on the first bus back to Jackson. Me and Tywain settled in his condo after he'd dropped his daughter off to his mother. He stayed in a nice lil spot on the east side of town. His condo was nice and relaxing. After going through all of what we had, it was a breath of fresh air.

I sat down on the couch and Princess sat on my lap. She kissed me on the cheek off and on. "I'm so glad that you're okay, Taurus, I'm not ready to lose you. I need you so bad," she said and laid her head in the crux of my neck.

Tywain paced back and forth rubbing his hands together. "It's time to get this money now, bro. I mean, we need to go hard. Now that I got a baby girl, I feel like I gotta have everything together by the time she get old enough to know what life is. We can't make no more mistakes, that's for damn sure."

I moved Princess off of me and she got a little attitude. I stood up and grabbed a Fruit Punch out of the refrigerator. "It's time to focus on The Rebirth then. Just because Nastia going through her little thing don't mean that our business with Hood Rich is shut down. He still fuckin' wit us the long way. We got another shipment of The Rebirth coming through on Tuesday. That's gone be the one."

"Yo, I done ran through all of our traps and they handling business. Them Comma Kids doing everything that we thought they was gone do. I'm proud. And ever since that one Gary situation got handed, we ain't had no problems out of the Mound, so that's a good thing."

Tywain nodded, "I wanna sew up Black Haven. I mean, shit popping in there already, but I wanna sew shit up so cold that everybody in that muhfucka shooting The Rebirth before this month is out. If they ain't shooting The Rebirth, then they blowing our Tropical Loud." He laughed, "Yo, I'm trying to have everybody from teens to seniors buying from us. We gotta get our money way the fuck up, and the only way to do it is to corner the market."

Princess came and wrapped her arms around me and laid her head on my chest. Tywain gave me a look that said she was clingy, and that I better be careful. But I didn't mind it. I was kinda falling for her anyway. It was something about her that made me feel good, and loved. I hadn't felt that in the past. So when she hugged all up on me, I never felt smothered. I felt like she genuinely cared about me, which was cool. I kissed her on the forehead. "You okay, lil momma?"

She nodded, "Yeah, I'm just a little tired. I ain't been able to sleep ever since you climbed out of the bed."

Tywain sat at the table and started to roll a blunt. "Yo, shit have been crazy as hell. Why don't y'all go in my room and get some sleep and I'll check on the traps. I should be back this way in about four hours. By that time, y'all should be well rested. But before I forget, what is your game plan with her. I mean, is she about to jump down wit us on this money shit, or is y'all just coolin'?"

"I don't know yet. That's something we can figure out a lil later. For now, I'm gone take you up on that rest."

Tywain left the condo about ten minutes later, and I jumped into his bed, after changing the sheets, prepared to get some much needed rest.

Then Princess came out of the bathroom in just a white bath towel and said, "I know you don't think you about to go to sleep for real because you not." She crumpled up her forehead.

"Oh yeah? Well what I'm about to do?" I asked, sitting on the edge of the bed and looking her up from toe to head.

She dropped the towel and seductively walked in between my legs. "You about to beat this pussy up. You know, pick up where you left off before you got called away on business."

She stuck two fingers into herself and fed them to me. I sucked those juices off of her fingers, and licked all around them. She tasted a little salty, and it drove me crazy.

I picked her little ass up and sat her on the edge of the bed. Squatting down between her legs, I watched her spread them wide for me.

"You gon' eat my pussy, baby? Huh? You gone make me come all over your tongue the way I been dreaming about?"

I took her right leg and put it on my shoulder. Spreading her sex lips apart, I noted how juicy they were. She had a pretty ass pussy. Not only were her outter lips fat and plump, but her inner lips were folded into the crease of her outter lips so that when I spread the outer ones, the inner ones stayed closed like a little rose. I took my tongue and opened them up, and saw so much pink that I damn near attacked her ass. There was nothing sexier to me than fat brown pussy lips, that exposed a bright pink background when you opened them up.

I slurped them lips into my mouth and threw her left leg over my shoulder, along with the right one. That made her bust that pussy wide open. I caught a faint whiff of that kitty smell and I felt the animal coming out of me. It wasn't nothing like the smell of pussy to me. If I could keep pussy up my nose all day long, I would.

As I sucked on her pussy lips, I slid my tongue into her little hole and she arched her back on the bed. "Shit, Taurus!" I stuck my tongue as deep into her as it would go, and then I ran it in circles around her vagina's nipple, before sucking that into my mouth, while I held her lips back with my thumbs.

She was going crazy on the bed, as her juices poured out of her and into my mouth. My entire chin was sticky, and I had the taste of her on my tongue. "I'm finna take over this pussy, Princess. When I'm done, you gon be *my* Princess, *my* baby girl."

"Okay, daddy. Whatever you say, just do it to me," she moaned with her eyes closed.

I grabbed the back of her knees with my hands and forced them to her chest. Then I just got real gross wit it. I got to licking from her asshole, all the way up to her clitoris, and then I would suck on her lips and pull them with my lips. I spread her pussy wide with my thumbs and tongue fucked the shit out of her while she squirmed all over the bed moaning like crazy.

"Taurus, I'm coming, Taurus! I'm coming!"

She started bucking into my face while I sucked on her clitoris as if I were a vampire. Her juices started squirting into my face, and I kept on sucking until she pushed my forehead away. "I can't take it no more! I can't take it!"

She tried to kick me away and jump off of the bed. I pulled her by her leg, and jumped on top of her, holding her down. I sucked into her neck, and then bit it.

"I'm bout to wear this lil pussy out."

I pulled my dick through the boxer hole and ran the fat head up and down in between her juicy sex lips. Her pussy was nice and hot. IIt felt so hot that it damn near scolded me. She tried to buck me from off the top of her. Her little legs kicked under me, and she pushed at my chest. "What you doin', Taurus? What you wanna do to me?"

I put my dick head right on her hole and slid a quarter of it in before she turned her hips and I slipped out of her. I got frustrated. "Stop playing wit me, Princess. Give me this muhfuckin' pussy before I take it from you!" I tried to put him back in, and once again as soon as the head went in partway, she turned her hips and I fell out of her.

"Nope, you ain't gettin' none of my goodies. If you want this shit, you gon' have to take it." She sat up and smacked my face. "Get the fuck off of me, nigga."

"Nigga?" I pushed her lil ass down to the bed and straddled her waist. Grabbing her by the neck, I squeezing my hand so tight that she closed her eyes. I could tell that I was hurting her a little bit and I didn't even care. I wanted to hit that ass, and that's what was going to happen. I threw all of my weight on to her, to the point she couldn't move, and then I took my dick and stuffed him all the way into her, pulled out partway, and slammed him back home.

At first she was struggling as if she was trying to get me off of her, but then she got to moaning at the top of her lungs.

"Yes. Yes. Fuck me, Taurus. Fuck me, daddy. As hard as you can," she growled into my ear as she scratched up my back, and held on to my waist.

I was long stoking that tight pussy and it was so good. I had never felt a pussy so wet, and snug at the same time. I was going so fast that all I could do was close my eyes, and tighten my stomach muscles. I came in her right away, and the pussy was so fire that I kept going. Ten minutes later, I came again when she screamed in my ear that she was coming.

Her pussy got to vibrating and sucking at me. I felt her nails dig into my back, and I didn't even care. It made me fuck her harder. I flipped her over and got out the bed, pulling her to the edge. I pulled her up to her knees, and entered her from the back while I grabbed a handful of her hair, spanking that ass at the same time. "Tell me I'm daddy. Tell me you gon' be a good girl."

"Aw, oh shit! You my daddy now. You my daddy! I'm gon' be a good girl for my daddy, I promise. I promise, daddy," she screamed as she smashed her ass back into me, and I beat that shit up. I came so many times in her that I didn't even remember how many, but I know she came more than I did.

Afterwards, we passed out. and by the time we woke up, it was two in the morning. She was still under me with her leg wrapped around my waist, and her arm cross my chest. I slid from under her and kissed her on the forehead. I slid on my boxers and stepped into the hallway, rubbing my eyes. I bumped right into Tywain.

"Damn, nigga, yo clumsy ass almost knocked me over," he said with a bottle of Hennessy in his hand. "Ah, nigga, guess who here?" He pointed to the living room.

I couldn't see who it was sitting on the couch perfectly from that angle. What I made out was a thick peanut butter thigh, and a red bottom heel.

He wrapped his arm around my shoulder. "Yo, that's Blaze in there kid. She just flew in from Houston and she dying to see you."

Chapter 14

Blaze was Tywain's cousin. We had met for the first time in Houston when my father had a sit down with a well connected drug dealer by the name of Jerry Walker. Me and her hit it off right away and spent damn near the entire time fucking like rabbits. Blaze was a famous stripper that went all over the United States as a featured dancer. She was about her paper, and she had strong feelings for me, even though we were just fuck buddies.

I went into the bathroom and gargled some of Tywain's scope while I pissed, and then showered. I slipped my Roberto Cavalli pants back on with my beater, and stepped into the living room.

As soon as she saw me, she bounced out of her seat and ran into my arms. "Taurus, baby, how have you been?"

Damn, she smelled good. I don't know what kind of perfume she had on but that shit smelled good. "I been busy like crazy, ma. But I'm okay." I hugged her, and took a step back.

She kissed me on each dimple. "I miss these dimples. I flew all the way from Houston just so I could kiss 'em."

"Thugs ain't supposed to have no damn dimples. That ain't gangsta," Tywain said, chugging from the bottle of liquor.

"Sound like you mad to me," Princess said, stepping into the living room in my big t-shirt. She looked Blaze up and down, and then extended her hand. "How you doin'? My name is Princess, and whats yours?"

Blaze looked down on her, and then over to me. She shook her hand. "My name is Blaze. I'm Tywain's cousin from Houston, Texas."

Princess nodded. "Okay, and what are you to him?" she asked, pointing in my direction with her head.

"Who, Taurus? Taurus just my friend. I mean, he's more than a friend, but we ain't got no papers on each other if that's what you trying to find out."

"I was. But that's just me being nosey because he my friend, too. But I care about him a lot, so if you're in his life, I just wanna get to know you because I'm here now and I ain't goin' nowhere no time soon. He's *my* daddy, and we just made that official, so." She kissed me on the cheek, and rubbed my chest.

"I'mma go get in the shower. I got *our* juices runnin' out of me. I'll be back in a few minutes." She kissed me again, all the while looking at Blaze.

Blaze frowned as she watched Princess walk to the bathroom and close the door. "Okay, that was rude. Where did you meet her at?"

I laughed, and shrugged my shoulders. "That's my lil baby right there. She from Jersey, by way of Haiti. You already know how they get down out there." I grabbed the bottle from Tywain and sipped out of it.

"Well, I done came a long way for this pipe." She grabbed my dick and squeezed it. "So sistah girl finna be real mad because this definitely ain't about to be no blank mission."

She gave me a look that said at least she hoped not.

I hugged her. "You bugging. That's just my lil baby. We ain't exclusive like that. She know what it is."

"I hope so because it sounded to me like she wasn't going. Like she was trying to let it be known that you belonged to her."

I wasn't about to feed into what Blaze was talking about. I was pretty sure that Princess wasn't on that. I mean, she was technically still Juice's girl. I didn't know where their relationship would go now that she knew he'd killed her brother, but that wasn't my business. I cared about her like a muhfucka, though, and she was a female that I could see myself chilling with for a long time. I didn't why I was so taken by her, but I was.

Tywain waved us off. "Why don't all three of y'all just go in my room and get it in?"

Blaze slapped her hand on her hip. "Damn, Tywain, I'm supposed to be yo cousin. That's how you gon' pimp me out?" She looked a little hurt.

He shrugged his shoulders. "Y'all gon' fuck anyway, so what's the matter wit smashin' both of them?"

"Because I want some of this all to myself. From what I can tell, she just had some. Now it's my turn. What's wrong with everybody gettin' they own turn?"

I laughed, and handed Tywain back the bottle. "We 'a figure all that out later."

"Yeah, and before we do, I wanna holla at you on some business that I think will make you very happy." She rubbed my chest. "Can we go out for a bite to eat? My treat."

One thing I liked about Blaze was the fact that she never minded spending her own money. She was one of those independent sistahs that liked to make it known. Every time I tried to buy her something, she didn't accept it. She once told me that she had enough men tricking on her, and she didn't see me as one of those types. She said she felt it was her business to keep me tip top, not the other way around. She said that I was a man that was supposed to have a female that was on top of her game at all costs. I had a hard time actually seeing what she saw in me, but I didn't argue with her logic.

After having a short dispute with Princess, I was able to make it out of the condo with Blaze. She had rented a Porsche truck. It was stylish. I sat in the passenger's seat with it all the way back.

"I just found out my daddy left me about fourteen properties, nine apartment buildings and five houses in Texas. The apartment buildings are all in Clover City."

I had no idea what Clover City was, or the reason why she was telling me what she was. But majority of the times she spoke about business, it was usually a lucrative opportunity for me.

"Where is Clover City, and why are you telling me all of this?" I asked putting my hand on her thick thigh. It felt hot and jiggled a little bit when I placed my hand on it. She was so fucking thick.

"Clover City is just like Englewood out of Chicago. It's a real big urban area where mostly Blacks and Latinos reside. The reason I am telling you about this is because I want to give you a few of those buildings for you to do your thing out of. Clover City is drug infested. Any Trap star that gets plugged in down there will make millions if they do it right. Now I've been in tune wit my cousin Tywain, and he was telling me about this Rebirth. He even sent me a sample of it. I watched one of the hustlers down there give it to a dope fiend, and the man went nuts. He got to begging Twin to give him more of it. Ever since that day, they been sweating me for that product."

"Okay, so what you want me to do?"

Two teenaged girls started fighting right outside of the truck. One girl was so fat that she was damn near busting out of her shoes. She grabbed the less chubby girl by her micro-braids and slung her to the ground. Then she got on top of her, punching her so many times in her face that my eyes started watering.

Blaze opened her truck door. "Should I get out and help that girl? She gon' kill her." She looked worried and afraid.

I pulled her back in. "Nall, what you can do is start the truck up and pull off." I pointed across the street. "You see all them girls running over here? They about to aid and assist her, trust me."

Blaze drove off just as the other girls loaded into the parking lot and turned it into a battle royal. "Damn, I wonder why our people hate each other so much."

"What do you mean?"

"I mean, I don't think I ever witnessed nothing like that with white folks. I'm pretty sure it happens occasionally, but it seems like we try and kill each other every day in our hoods. So I wonder why we hate each other so much?"

"I don't think it's that we hate each other. I think we all just try and protect the land that we consider ours. From way back when, we've only had so very little. We were forced to keep up and slave over the white man's land so much that when we were finally able to get our own little pieces of land, or territories, we protected them with our lives. So I think it's just ingrained in us to be violent and aggressive on our turfs. I mean, I don't know, at least that's how I feel. But I want better than all of this. I can't see myself settling and never leaving the hood."

"Me neither, I got big dreams. I want to move out of the United States period, and move over to Japan, or Australia. Both of those places are pretty peaceful. I'd move to Japan for all of the modern technology. Not to mention, its so laid back there. I went and visited for two weeks. It was amazing. The people are so nice and inviting. I didn't want to leave. The food was also the best."

"Okay, I can get that. But why Australia?"

"Well I'm an exotic dancer. The dancer's over there make a pretty penny. The men over there love the color of my skin, and my body drives them crazy. They pay top dollar to watch me do my thing. It's pretty cool. I stayed there for a week, and I felt well respected."

She got on to the highway and punched the gas. "When me and you gon' travel together?" I asked running my hand under her short skirt. She was wearing some tight panties, but I easily snuck my fingers into her leg hole and on to that bald kitty. Her sex lips were thick, and meaty. I separated them with my two fingers and slid my middle one deep into her hole. It felt hot and moist.

She moaned, and sucked on her bottom lip. "Taurus, I would travel the world with you right now if you wanted to. I'm not kidding. We can go to the Airport right now, and fly to Japan, and start from there and hit up every continent on earth. I'd pay for everything, just as long as you pipe me down whenever I tell you to, and even when I don't." She spread her right leg wide, as I started to go to town on her with my three fingers. Her pussy was making so much noise from being so wet that it sounded like I was fingering a bowl of pudding.

She stepped on the gas harder and the truck shot forward topping speeds of a hundred miles an hour. I leaned my head into her lap and ate that pussy like a maniac. It didn't take long for her to come. I wiped my mouth on her thick thigh, and told her that I was gone beat that shit up before she left.

We wound up parked at the Mississippi bridge that overlooked the city.

"Okay, now back to what I was saying. The reason I want you to take over Clover City is because I'm familiar with all of the power players over there. My father had plugs in and out of law enforcement. A lot of the property over there is mine, and if you can go on a two year run, we'd have enough money to take you out of the game. Then we could flip it and wash it clean by opening a few businesses. I'm not far from getting my real estate license. Once I do that, I want to sell real estate to influential people while at the same time acquiring property that is of value to the white man, suburban property, and things of that nature. I'll stand behind you one hundred percent, and put you in with all of the power players. The only thing I ask of you is that after the two year run, you and I travel the world together." She looked me in the eye.

"Let me think about that. But as if right now. All of that sound real good to me. Ever since you be in my life, all you've been is a positive. I feel like at the very least I owe you some travel time."

"Oh you think that's all, huh?" She straddled my lap, and pulled her panties off of her ankle, and we fucked right there overlooking the city.

When she dropped me back off over Tywain's house, he was coming out of the door with a look on his face that said he was on business. I kissed Blaze, and she told me she would be in touch once she got everything situated. She didn't even ask Tywain what was wrong, she pulled off, and blew the horn twice. I caught up to him before hie got in his car.

"Yo, what's good, nigga? Why you looking like you about to go kill something?"

"I am. This bitch nigga done put his hands on my lil cousin for the last time. She in the hospital right now, and this nigga at the crib with my lil cousins like it's all good. I'm bout to show this nigga what it do, though."

He opened his door and got in and I jumped in the passenger's seat. We were about to pull off when I saw Princess running out of the building. "Yo, nigga, hold up."

"Bro, I just told you I'm about to kill this nigga. You sure you want her wit us when I do this?"

It was too late to give him an answer because she opened the back door and got in. "I already know what you about to do and I'mma be right there when you do it. I hate niggas that beat females anyway, so if you really wanna get back at this nigga you'll let me kill his ass," she said, holding the back of our seats.

When we got into Tywain's cousin's hospital room, she was sleeping. He woke her up by squeezing her thigh. Her head had swollen up to the size of a black pumpkin. Both of her eyes were black, and nearly stuck closed. Her lips were busted, and she had a cast on both arms, and a neck brace. After seeing all of that, I wanted to kill the nigga that did all of that to her.

Her name was Jennifer, and from what I knew about her, she was a sweetheart. She was very religious. She was also very polite and kind. Every time we met, she gave me a hug and told me that Jesus loved me. She always found a way to compliment me on something. She drove the Memphis city bus. She had three little girls, and her mother also stayed in the house with her.

She looked up at Tywain, and groaned in pain. "Hey, cousin, it's good to see you."

I saw tears drop from the homey's eyes. "No the fuck it ain't, Jennifer. I don't like seeing you in this hospital like this." He knelt down and kissed her on the forehead.

"It's okay, Tywain. Everybody has to go through things like this. It's just my time. Pretty soon it'll all be better, and we'll all be smiling."

"What happened this time, Jennifer? Why did he do this to you?" he asked, shifting his weight from one foot to the other.

She shrugged her shoulders. "I don't want to dwell on it. What's done is done. I just ain't gone make no more mistakes. At least I'mma try not to. The good Lord sho did say that ain't nobody perfect."

Tywain grabbed her hand. "Tell me what you did wrong?"

Jennifer closed her eyes. I could tell that she was in pain. I didn't know if Tywain was squeezing her hand or not, but he was definitely doing something. "He beat me because he want my baby to sleep in the room with him at nights now. He say she old enough to sleep wit her daddy and that I don't need to be in the bed. She only eight, and I told him that she ain't supposed to be sleeping in no bed with him in just her panties. He slapped me so hard that at first I forgot what I had said to him until I got up and seen my baby still in the bed looking scared as a small animal in front of a Lion."

Tywain looked over his shoulder at me, and curled his lip. "So then what happened?"

"Well after that, I try and get Hannah out of the room, but he grabbed me by my neck and threw me against the wall. It knocked me right out. When I woke up the door was closed and locked. I could hear my baby in there huffing and puffing, and sometimes screaming. I took that to mean that he was hurting her so I broke the door down and attacked him with the broom. I whacked him right across his back wit the handle. I sho did. He ran out of that room so fast that smoke came from his feet. I grabbed my naked baby, and was on my way out of the house when he grabbed me by my hair, and threw me to the floor. He beat me so bad that even while I was knocked out I was feeling the pain."

Tywain stood up and kissed her on the forehead. "That shit is unacceptable. I ain't geeing for it. I told you before that if he ever put his hands on you again, I was gone body his ass, right?"

"I don't think it gotta come to all of that, though, do it, Tywain?"

"Right! Now I told you that if he ever touch one of my little cousins, I was gone kill his ass. This bitch nigga doing more than that. He beating yo ass, and fucking on Hannah. What you think I'm supposed to do?"

"We gotta put this in God's hands. Let the good Lord deal wit him, because it's not for us to." She tried to reach out and touch him.

He yanked his arm away. "Let the good Lord handle it?" He curled up his upper lip, and frowned. "Well let me ask you something. Did you pray about this already?"

"I sure did. I talked to Jesus just before I went to sleep and I asked him to rescue my family from the devil that was tryin to take it over."

Tywain smiled, "You know what? I think He heard you, because He sent me. I'm gone be the one to rescue you from that devil in that house, me and my angels." He waved his hand over me and Princess.

Chapter 15

I took two steps back, and then with all of my might I kicked in the door, and it flew open and hung part way off of its hinges. Calvin looked like he was about to shit on himself when he saw us run into the house straight at him as he sat on the couch with Hannah on his lap. She was only in her panties, and that pissed me off because I got to imagining that being Mary.

Princess came and snatched the girl off of his lap, and Tywain punched him so hard that his head hit the wall in back of the couch. Before he could absorb that blow, he hit him with another one that knocked a tooth out of his mouth. I picked him up and dumped him on his neck, right on the glass table. He fell through it and tried to crawl.

"Tywain, Taurus, why y'all doin' this to me, man? I ain't did shit to y'all."

I grabbed him by his neck and pulled him to his feet. Getting behind him, I led him down into the basement. "Princess, get the girls dressed and take them out to the car. Drive them to his Aunty house and come back here. She already expecting you. Now go," I demanded. I was ready to get into his ass. That was one nigga I was looking forward to killing.

When we got him to the basement, Tywain smacked the shit out of him. I punched him straight in his right eye and dumped him on his back, hard. He bounced off the concrete and everything.

"Bitch nigga, you think you gone keep beating on my cousin? I'mma show yo ass something." He came up with a hammer. "Hold this bitch nigga down."

He tried to run, I caught him by the back of his shirt, and punched him in the side of the jaw. Then I swept my leg under him, dropping him on his ass. He fell and hit the back of his head.

I handcuffed his hands behind his back, threw him back on the floor, and sat on his stomach while Tywain pulled his socks off.

"Bitch nigga, you wanna make my people go through pain? Well I got something fo that ass." He held his foot steady, raised the hammer, and brought it down at full speed, smashing his big toe to the point it splattered in blood.

Calvin hollered so loud that it hurt my ears. "Aw shit! What the fuck! What the fuck I do to you, Tywain? This shit ain't right!" His mouth was full of blood. It ran from his nose as well.

I smacked the shit out of him. "Shut yo punk ass up! Bitch nigga, you wanna beat women and rape kids? Fuck this nigga over, bro!"

Tywain brought the hammer down again and smashed the next toe, and then the next one, until every toe on his foot looked like it had been ran over by a car. He handed me the salt, and I poured it all over his foot, and he screamed like I imagined Jennifer screamed while he was beating her.

Princess came down the basement steps and stood over us. "This him right here, huh?" She looked disgusted. "So you like to beat women, huh?"

He shook his head. "No. I'm sorry. Please save me. I'm so sorry."

"Let me see that hammer, Tywain." He handed it to her and she pulled me off of him. "Hold that nigga down, both of y'all. Hurry up before he pass out." She took a step back. "And turn him on his side."

"On his side? What the fuck you on?" Tywain started.

170

"Just do it," she hollered, putting her hair into a pony tail. As soon as he was on his side, she pulled down his boxers, and pulled his dick out. Holding it in her hand, she said, "I hate niggas that like to hurt lil kids. That makes you a predator to me, and this is what you predators deserve." She raised the hammer way over her head, and brought it down with all of her might right on to his dick head. It smashed into the concrete. She raised the hammer and did it again, hitting the same spot. Blood splattered everywhere.

He passed out, and I smacked the shit out of him. "Get yo punk ass up. This shit ain't over. Hit em again, lil momma."

This time she started beating his meat with the hammer. She went on a rampage until his member was hanging on by a thin piece of skin. Tywain stepped on it and pulled it off with the bottom of his shoe. I could see the blood pouring out of his private area hole. Every time he passed out, I woke his ass back up. There was blood all over the basement floor.

It ended with us burning his body in a metal garbage can right there in the basement. Then we took his bones and beat them into dust, finally pouring them into the creek. It took us three hours to mop up all that blood and sanitize the whole basement, and living room. Afterward we went and got pizza and ate it at Tywain's house. I felt a lot better, and I could tell that Tywain did too because he was cracking jokes about how Calvin was screaming every time Princess brought that hammer down.

That night, Princess told me that she wanted to kill Juice, and she wanted to know what I thought about it. "I mean, I know he yo brother and all, but what you gotta realize is that he killed my family, and he played wit my head. I know you wouldn't ever go for no shit like that. So I don't think it would be fair if you expected me to."

Tywain must've overheard us talking in the guest room cause he knocked on the door and opened it with a smile on his face.

"I mean, I was on my way to the bathroom and I just so happened to hear her saying what she said about Juice. Now it's not my business in particular, but I just wanted to let y'all know what my thoughts was in regards to all of this."

Princess laughed. "You sound like one of them old black actors from the forties when they were playing roles of an idiot." She shook her head. "But what are your thoughts?"

"On some real shit, seeing as this nigga didn't get no consequences from what happened to my daughter and your son, I feel like she got a right to do whatever she wanna do, and it ain't for us to stop her. We already see that she got hella heart. And you lost a whole ass son because of Juice. He should pay the price with his life." He curled his upper lip. "On some real shit, if she didn't do it, I was gone have a hard time not doing it because I hate that nigga. No disrespect to you and your family, either."

" None taken." I didn't know how I felt about them discussing the murder of my brother. It was no secret that we had bad blood between one another, I just didn't know if it was so bad that I wanted to see him in the dirt. I just didn't know how I felt.

Princess sat on my lap, and kissed my cheek. "What's wrong, daddy? You ain't saying nothing, and that usually mean that you're feeling some type of way."

Tywain frowned. "Bro, I know you ain't actually having feelings for this nigga again. This nigga done got yo son killed, my baby momma killed, Shaneeta shot the fuck up, tortured, and then killed, my daughter cut out of her momma stomach, and then he killed Pac Man, and had the audacity to fuck his sister, knowing that he killed her brother. Yo, that nigga grimey as a muthafucka. I wish you give me the green light and I'll torture that nigga worse than we did Calvin. My baby wasn't even born before that fool brought fire down on her head. Now, because of him, she ain't got no mother, and you ain't got no brother," he concluded, pointing at Princess.

"Yo, chill, Tywain. Yo words starting to sting a lil bit. We all know that nigga fucked us all in one way or the other, but you ain't gotta be rubbing that shit in like lotion." Princess rolled her eyes. "His time gone come because that's just how karma work, whether Taurus want it to happen or not." She laid her head on my chest.

"I wash my hands of it all. Whatever happens, happens. I just know my mother gon' be fucked up about it. I'm surprised she ain't been going nuts over my other brother. But then again, that nigga was so disrespectful to her that she probably don't even miss him."

"Have she ever asked you about him?" Tywain asked, smoking on a cigarette. He plopped down on the couch, and sighed.

"Nall," I shook my head and rubbed Princess' back.

"Then she probably already know. She just don't give a fuck about that lil nigga. Dude was another special case, bro. I never hit it off wit none of yo brothers. They just some type of way."

"I miss mine. He may not have been the best brother in the world but he was all I had. He wanted me to come

173

down here so I could have a better life. Its fucked up to know that he was dead before I even got here, and his murderer was the nigga to embrace me first. That shit crazy. He really trying to live up to his name." She stood on her tippy toes and kissed my lips, before sitting down on the couch and crossing her legs.

"What you mean by that?" Tywain asked, trying to pass her the cigarette.

She pushed his hand out of her face with her eyes closed. "Ugh, I hate cigarettes. That shit so nasty to me, and they stink." She opened her mouth and stuck her tongue out, pointing a finger down her throat to emphasize her point.

Tywain waved her off. "Anyway, tell me what you meant by the whole name thing?"

"You remember in the movie when Bishop kilt Raheim, and he still showed up at the funeral hugging all of his family and shit? That's basically what Juice did to me. It's just he went a whole lot further wit it. "She frowned her face in anger. "Damn, I'm so stupid."

I slid onto the couch beside her and put her head on my chest. "It's good. Stop killing yourself over this. Everything gone work itself out. Trust me on that."

Tywain smiled and blew a cloud of smoke to the ceiling. "I know it is if I got anything to do wit it. I can't take this shit lying down. That nigga nearly had my daughter killed. I done fucked over plenty niggas for far less. I feel like gettin knocked on a hum bug, and going in there and bodying his ass myself. If you ask me, that nigga should've been dead."

I held Princess more firm, as I felt her tears drop on to my arm. I could tell that she was hurting, and if I could have, I would have done anything to wash away that pain inside of her.

***

The next day, I awoke to find her pacing back and fortt inside of the room. We had screwed all night long. I made slow passionate love to her while she cried her little heart out. The last thing I remembered before I passed out was her telling me that she would be okay, and that she was thankful that I had been there to heal her. But as I looked at her from the bed, she looked like something was definitely wrong with her. I sat all the way up, and she acted as if she didn't even notice until I stretched my arms over my head, and yawned.

She stopped in her tracks. "Good morning, baby. How are you feeling?" She crawled into the bed and kissed me on the lips, before laying her head on my chest. It seemed like she loved to do that.

"I'm more concerned about you. Tell what's going on inside of your head?" I wrapped both of my arms around her, and held her close.

"I just been thinking about my brother, and the whole Juice thing. For some reason, I can't get it out of my head. I got to thinking about how it would feel to kill him, and to be honest, I don't think it would make me feel any better. I think it would only make me feel worse than I already do because it would cause so much heartache and pain on your family. I don't know what would have made Juice do wat he did to my brother, but I do know that karma is a bitch, and one day   she's gonna shit all over him."

She looked up and kissed   me on the neck. "I'm so thankful for you though. Ever since you've been a part of my life, you've made me feel so special. The only thing I ask is that you never turn your back on me, and that you always be there for me, please."

"I got you. You just keep on being you and I'll take care of everything else. I promise you that." I kissed her on the forehead. "Is there anything else you worried about?"

She sat up and looked me in the eye. "Yeah, but I don't want you to get mad if I tell you exactly what's on my heart. Can you at least promise me that?"

I nodded. "Tell me what's good?"

She took a deep breath. "Okay, now you kinda told me what your reason was for not settling down wit Shakia. You said she was too clingy and that she didn't respect you when you told her that you wasn't ready to settle down wit just one female. So now my thing is this, I'm starting to feel some strong feelings for you, and I don't know what to do about them because I don't want to run you off. But at the same time, I don't want to be holding them in all the time. The bottom line is that I want to be wit you. Now I'm not trying to stop you from doing you just yet, but that's definitely on my agenda down the road. So I guess my question to you is, is there a chance that you and me can be together the way I feel like we should be?" She laid her hand on my chest and started rubbing downward toward my exposed abs.

I cared about her a lot, and I didn't even know why my feelings were so strong for her, but they were. Out of all of the females I had been with, I felt like she was the one I could see myself wifing one day. "You know what, Princess, I can't really promise you that I'm ready to settle down and just be with one person. But what I can promise you is that if you give me time and not pressure me, I will get there. I mean, you my lil baby. I'm crazy as hell over you. And if I was to be with any one female, it would definitely be you."

She turned all the way around and looked me in the eye. "Are you sure about that?" She grasped my chin inside of her lil hand and tilted it upward so she could see my eyes more clearly.

I nodded. "Yeah, I mean that."

"Okay, so what does that make us right now, because I wanna be your woman?"

"Right now, I say we don't even put a title to it. I say we just keep doing what we been doing. We take things as they come and see where it goes."

She kissed my lips again. "Well, I'm telling you now that in my mind you're my daddy, and I'm crazy about you. I know I gotta share you wit other females for the time being, but very soon I'm hoping we'll get to a better place where it's just you and me." She snuggled into my chest again. "Hey, can we got for a drive?"

" Yeah, let me hop into the shower." As I got out of the bed, I heard the sound of five loud ass gunshots, followed by a loud ass *boom*, as if something had blown up. I heard a series of more gunfire, and then there was a loud *boom* again, but that time it sounded like it was right outside of the bedroom. I pushed Princess down to the floor. Then I reached under the bed and came up with my Mach .90. I cocked it, and looked down at Princess. "You stay in here I'm about to go out here and see what's going on."

As soon as I said the last part, I heard another series of gunfire that sounded so close it made my ears ring. I opened the bedroom door and crouched low to the floor. More gunfire was sounded off, and then I heard our front door bust open, and more gunshots ensued.

Boom! Boom! Boom!

"Bitch ass niggas," I heard Tywain say, and then I heard more shots fire.

That told me that the horney was under fire. I ran into the hallway, and ducked low to the floor. I could see Tywain on his back shooting at the doorway. There was a fat dude with an Obama mask on getting hit up all in his chest and neck. I mean Tywain lit his ass up. He had on a black t-shirt, and it turned red real fast, with big holes in it.

Another dude bent the corner, and before he could up his toolie, I chopped him up with the Mach, running right at him and squeezing the trigger. My bullets knocked him backward, and made his face explode. I stood over him and popped him three more times in the face to over kill his ass. I looked down the stairs and there was another dude on his way up, but when he saw me, he shot in my direction twice and then ran outside to the car that was waiting for him. I tried to chase his ass down spraying the Mach. But he was too fast. He dove into the backseat of the car, and it sped off down the street with me chasing behind it like a mad man.

When they turned the corner, I finally stopped. When I got back into the house, I damn near broke down crying because there was my right hand man, lying in the middle of the floor, in Princess's arms, shaking in a puddle of blood.

It looked like he had taken more than five shots to the mid-section. I fell to my knees with tears in my eyes.

"Taurus, come on, we gotta get him to a hospital right now, or he gone die." She put her hand over one of the holes in his chest that was pouring out blood. It oozed through her fingers.

I was shell shocked. I literally could not move. I just envisioned us burying him, and I could not move. It was like the whole world had stopped. I saw Princess's mouth moving but I couldn't hear a word that was corning out of it.

Finally, she crawled across the floor and smacked the shit out of me. I think it had more of a physical effect because she had blood on her hands. But she hit me so hard that it knocked some sense into me. "Get the fuck up, and lets get him to the hospital, now!"

The next thing I remember was us putting him in the back seat of my truck, and me speeding away from the curb. I don't even know how we made it to the hospital one hundred percent, I just know we did. I grabbed a wheel chair, and we placed him into it, and then grabbed a white nurse lady, and told her he had been shot to get him help. She nodded her head and wheeled him inside.

Me and Princess jumped back into my truck and sped away. There were so many things going through my mind that I couldn't even think straight. I didn't recognize neither one of the dudes that had been airing at us, them nor the car they were driving, so it could have been anybody. The worst drama to have in the world was drama with somebody that you didn't even know you were beefing with.

"Fuck. I hope he make it. How is we gone find out if he made it or not?" Princess screamed. "And who the fuck was that anyway?" She had tears rolling down her cheeks, and her nose was running.

"I don't know, baby. Fuck. I don't know. But we can't go back to his crib and find out. We gotta get the fuck out of Memphis for a little while."

"And go where? Where are we gonna go, Taurus? Everything you got going on, its going on in Memphis. This where all yo money at."

She had a point right there. But I knew the heat was about to come down. There was no way that the police wasn't finna be on our ass. Tywain's house was a murder scene, and we had left two dead bodies there. We had to get the fuck out of Memphis, and as fast as possible.

"It just seem like ever since I got down here, so much shit been going on. First my brother, then all of those other people, and now Tywain." She broke into a fit of tears.

I waited until I pulled up at a stop light, and pulled her over to me. I wrapped her in my arms. "Baby, we just gotta get the fuck up outta here, and we'll figure everything else out later on. You know I-"

Boom. Somebody crashed into the back of my truck so hard that it made me slam my head on the steering wheel, causing the airbag to deploy. Princess fell out of my arms and down under her seat.

"What the fuck was that?" she hollered.

A van pulled up on the side of us, and the side door opened. The shooters didn't waste no time unloading their fully automatic weapons.

Pop! Pop! Pop! Boom! Boom! Boom!

My driver's side window shattered, and so did the window that Princess was sitting at. It felt like the car was being pushed over by the gunfire. I dropped to the floor, and pushed on the gas with my hand, making the truck lunge forward into traffic, and the bullets kept on coming at full blast. As soon as the truck got a little ways away from the shooters, I got up and into the driver's seat, and was smacked in the shoulder by a hot one. It felt like somebody had poured acid directly on to my skin and it dropped inside of me. "Aw shit," I hollered, and then a bullet hit the front windshield, and it shattered, falling into my lap. I pressed my foot on to the pedal, and stormed away at full speed with the wind blowing into my face. My shoulder was killing me. But the bullets kept coming.

"Taurus, are you okay?" Princess asked from the floor of the passenger's side. She had glass all in her hair, and I could see little cuts and specks of blood on her forehead.

I made a right turn and wound up on the sidewalk, flying down it at full speed. The people that were walking on it saw my truck coming and jumped out of the way. I crashed into a stand of watermelons and kept on going. A lot of them fell right into my open windshield, and into my lap.

Princess did the best she could to clear them away. The brown van was driving down the street with the side door open still airing at us like it was the most normal thing in the world. I kept feeling bullets slamming into my driver's side door, and more than once they flew past my head. I could feel the air of them.

Princess grabbed my Mach, and climbed into the backseat of the truck, just as the window back there shattered. She waited for it to stop, and then she pointed the Mach out of the window and pulled the trigger, sending multiple bullets their way.

"Leave us alone, you muthafuckas, " she said, and pulled the trigger again and again. The van swerved into oncoming traffic and smashed into a car head on. I took advantage of that diversion and sped away from the scene, doing damn near a hundred miles an hour. I was starting to feel woozy. I knew that I was losing a lot of blood. My vision got cloudy.

The next thing I knew, I was being smacked on the face and I awoke to see Princess behind the wheel. "Stay woke, baby, we're almost there. I just need you to hold on for a little while longer. Please don't die on me. I need you, baby. Please!"

I did everything I could to keep my eyes open, but no matter how hard I tried, I just could not do it. I felt sleepier than I ever had in my whole entire life. So as I was nodding to let her know that I understood what she was saying, I passed back out.

When I awoke the next time, I was in a hospital bed. but I wasn't in a hospital room, at least it didn't seem like I was. The room was dark, and it was all concrete. It looked almost like I was in a basement of some sort. I looked down at my arms and saw that I had an IV leading from a machine directly into them. I looked down at my shoulder and noted that it was patched up, yet there was a big blood stain on it. I tried to move it and couldn't. I felt a little pain, but it wasn't as bad as it had been before I passed out. I tried to sit up, but I got dizzy right away.

"Baby, take it easy," Princess said. And for the first time, I noticed that she'd been sitting on the side of me the whole time.

She shot to her feet when she saw that I was awake. "Grandma. Grandma, he woke. I need you down here right away," she hollered, looking toward the stairs that I was now able to make out.

My vision was still a little blurry, and I couldn't visually process much. My mouth felt dry and I felt so confused. I didn't know where I was, or how I had gotten there.

A short dark-skinned woman came down the stairs and stood over me. She said something in a foreign language, and then shook her head. "You're going to be okay, my baby boy. I patched you up pretty good. There shouldn't be no more problems with that there shoulder of yours. You lost a lot of blood, but the bottom line is that you're gonna make it. Lucky for you my granddaughter is your same blood type."

My eyes felt heavy as hell. I tried to keep them open, but it was becoming harder and harder to do. I felt weak, and sick all at the same time. "How long have I been down here?"

Princess came over and put her hand on my chest. "Baby, you been laying in this bed for two weeks now. Every time you wake up, you fall right back to sleep. I think it's because you lost so much blood. You didn't just get shot in your shoulder either. She lowered her head. "You got shot in your shoulder and twice in yo back. You lost a whole lot of blood, but my grandma did her thing for us. It's a blessing." She rubbed my forehead and then kissed me on it.

"What's up wit Tywain?"

"He pulled through, but you already know that them boys was all over him. Right now, he still in the hospital and they got him handcuffed to the bed. I guess the best news in all of that is the fact that he pulled through because, for a minute, I didn't think that he would. He got shot over nine times. They don't know the exact count because some of the bullets went into the same holes, and some of them went straight through. I just thank God that he's alive and well. We can always get him a lawyer. They put on the news that it was gang related and that the shooters are still on the run. I already torched your truck, and had it broken down into little biddy pieces. My uncle Chewy did us that favor." She wrapped her arm over me and hugged me. "I'm so glad that you okay, baby. I need you so much. I don't know what this life without you would be like."

I stayed in that basement for an entire two months before I was strong enough to make it out of that bed. As crazy as it seemed, the police still didn't have me and Princess' pictures posted. I didn't understand why they didn't, but I guess that meant that the homey was holding up his end like a G.

Gary, Deion, and Martell kept shit real, and kept our organization flourishing. Since Hood Rich had met up with me and Tywain on a few occasions and saw Gary with us, they took my word to keep doing business with him while I was down. I guess word got back to them about what had happened, and they was more than cool wit keeping shit moving with our lil homies. I did a lot of business over the phone, using code words, directing Gary on how to handle shit, and he listened like his life depended on it. I guess that it did.

The Rebirth was making a killing all through the city. It had our pockets sitting real nice. Our Comma Kids were bringing me bags of money, and I was having Princess fuck wit the businesses, and turning the money over. The large sums that she turned over, I shipped straight out to our Swiss accounts and the few we'd acquired in the Cayman Islands.

My mother got to doing her thing so hard down in Jackson that not only did she open up a Salon, but she opened up three restaurants, and two clothing stores. My lil cousins and them were deep into the Hip Hop world, so I allowed her to put some money behind them. They started their own record label, and got signed on with Priority Records. They got a multi-million dollar deal.

Any move that I could bust while I was down in that basement, I did. After the second month, I was restless, and I was ready to get the fuck from down there. I was stronger, and I had full mobility in my left shoulder, and my back no longer felt all stiff.

We heard that they had moved Tywain to the county jail. They were holding him on a probation violation since they couldn't get him on nothing else. I made sure that Princess hit his books heavily. He had to at least have about twenty racks on his account and we snatched him up a five thousand dollar lawyer to help him fight his revocation proceedings. Jennifer had his daughter and we made sure that he didn't have to worry about her being taken care of. We made sure that Jennifer got ten gees every week, and we personally picked her up and took her shopping as much as possible. I made sure that we covered all bases when it came to him.

Me and Princess decided to move out into a part of Memphis called West Allis. It was a low key suburban duck off where mostly doctors and lawyers stayed with their families. I felt that I needed to lay low for a little while, and at the same time, keep my eye on our growing business because The Rebirth was doing its thing like crazy, even our Meth houses were doing numbers. We were able to fall back for a full year without there being any hassle.

Our names had still not popped up in the news so I was feeling like maybe we were gone be okay. I started to feel real optimistic, so much so that I put a baby in Princess. She wound up giving birth to our baby girl six months after we moved to West Allis. I was so happy that I didn't know what to do with myself. Our little girl came out so beautiful. She looked just like her mother, but she had my deep dimples. Seeing my daughter for the first time was almost too much for me. I mean, I broke down because I had always wanted a daughter and she was perfect to me in every single way.

I spent the first three months of her life carrying her around the house everywhere I went. I don't think I took my eyes off of her for more than five minutes at a time anytime that I was awake. When it came time for her to be fed, I didn't even look to Princess to do that. I jumped up and did it right away.

Every night that she woke up crying, I was the first out of the bed and to her side, taking her out of the crib and carrying her around the house until she fell back to sleep. I changed her and bathed her all on my own. Princess told me that if I didn't ease up, I was going to   spoil her. But I didn't care because that was definitely the plan. I had to say that just having my daughter and Princess up under me all the time made me the happiest man on earth. I actually started to feel fulfilled, and then it happened.

It was our daughter's one year birthday, and me and Princess thought that we would do something small for her because we were still laying low and trying to skate under the radar. So we threw her a family birthday party and invited my mother, my sister, and a few of the family from down in Jackson.

We bought our daughter two huge birthday cakes and a tub of vanilla ice cream, along with pizza and buffalo wings. I put some music on and we made it a family affair. I spent some time with my mother, and we had a nice long talk. She brought me up to speed with everything that was taking place in Jackson. She was doing quite well and I was proud of her, to say the least. After our talk, we slow danced together, and I did the same thing with my sister.

I mean, everything was going good, until later on that night after everybody besides my mother and sister had left to go home. They had made a mess of our house and my mother and sister were helping me and Princess get our home back in order. It took us two whole hours to get it back clean. By the time we finished, it was one in the morning. I had just finished tying the garbage bags up, preparing to take them outside, when our daughter Jahliyah started throwing up. She had eaten so much cake that I guess her little body couldn't handle it. I picked her up and rushed her into the bathroom, where I allowed her to keep vomiting over the toilet before I washed her up and got her ready for bed.

I was coming out of her bedroom, and walking into the living room when I noticed that everybody was staring straight ahead as if they were in a trance. I didn't know what was going on until I actually stepped all the way into the living room, and what I saw made my heart damn near jump out of my chest.

There was my father, in a three piece Armani suit. He had a Gold .45 in one hand, and my mother by the throat with his other one. She was up against the wall on her tippy toes, and he had the gun inside of her mouth, with Juice standing right behind him.

When he saw me, he smiled like a maniac. "You got the nerve to try and take over my family, and fuck my wife. This is about to be a night that you will never forget, I can promise you that."

Juice took his twin .40 calibers and pointed one at me, and the other one at Princess. "I'm gon' enjoy this shit, Pops." He smiled as I saw his finger caress the trigger.

To Be Continued...
Raised As A Goon 3
Coming Soon

BOW DOWN TO MY GANGSTA

By **Ca$h & Jamaica**

TORN BETWEEN TWO

By **Coffee**

BLOOD OF A BOSS **IV**

By **Askari**

BRIDE OF A HUSTLA **III**

THE FETTI GIRLS **III**

By **Destiny Skai**

WHEN A GOOD GIRL GOES BAD **II**

By **Adrienne**

LOVE & CHASIN' PAPER **II**

By **Qay Crockett**

THE HEART OF A GANGSTA **II**

By **Jerry Jackson**

TO DIE IN VAIN **II**

By **ASAD**

LOYAL TO THE GAME **IV**

By **TJ & Jelissa**

A DOPEBOY'S PRAYER **II**

By **Eddie "Wolf" Lee**

A HUSTLER'S DECEIT **III**

THE BOSS MAN'S DAUGHTERS **III**

BAE BELONGS TO ME **II**

By **Aryanna**

TRUE SAVAGE **II**

By **Chris Green**

RAISED AS A GOON **III**

By **Ghost**

IF LOVING YOU IS WRONG…

By **Jelissa**

BLOODY COMMAS

By **T.J.**

Available Now

(CLICK TO PURCHASE)

RESTRAINING ORDER **I & II**

By **CA$H & Coffee**

LOVE KNOWS NO BOUNDARIES **I II & III**

By **Coffee**

RAISED AS A GOON

By **T.J.**

LAY IT DOWN **I & II**

LAST OF A DYING BREED

By **Jamaica**

LOYAL TO THE GAME

LOYAL TO THE GAME II

LOYAL TO THE GAME III

By **TJ & Jelissa**

PUSH IT TO THE LIMIT

By **Bre' Hayes**

BLOOD OF A BOSS **I II & III**

By **Askari**

THE STREETS BLEED MURDER **I, II & III**

THE HEART OF A GANGSTA

By **Jerry Jackson**

CUM FOR ME

CUM FOR ME 2

CUM FOR ME 3

An **LDP Erotica Collaboration**

BRIDE OF A HUSTLA **I & II**

THE FETTI GIRLS **I & II**

By **Destiny Skai**

WHEN A GOOD GIRL GOES BAD

By **Adrienne**

A GANGSTER'S REVENGE **I II III & IV**

THE BOSS MAN'S DAUGHTERS

THE BOSS MAN'S DAUGHTERS II

A SAVAGE LOVE **I & II**

BAE BELONGS TO ME

A HUSTLER'S DECEIT I, II

By **Aryanna**

A KINGPIN'S AMBITON

A KINGPIN'S AMBITION **II**

By **Ambitious**

TRUE SAVAGE

By **Chris Green**

A DOPEBOY'S PRAYER

By **Eddie "Wolf" Lee**

WHAT ABOUT US **I & II**

NEVER LOVE AGAIN

THUG ADDICTION

By **Kim Kaye**

THE KING CARTEL **I, II & III**

By **Frank Gresham**

THESE NIGGAS AIN'T LOYAL **I, II & III**

By **Nikki Tee**

GANGSTA SHYT **I II &III**

By **CATO**

THE ULTIMATE BETRAYAL

By **Phoenix**

BOSS'N UP **I & II**

By **Royal Nicole**

I LOVE YOU TO DEATH

By Destiny J

<u>I RIDE FOR MY HITTA</u>
<u>I STILL RIDE FOR MY HITTA</u>
By **Misty Holt**
<u>LOVE & CHASIN' PAPER</u>
By **Qay Crockett**
<u>TO DIE IN VAIN</u>
By **ASAD**

<u>BOOKS BY LDP'S CEO, CA$H</u>

(CLICK TO PURCHASE)

<u>TRUST IN NO MAN</u>

<u>TRUST IN NO MAN 2</u>

<u>TRUST IN NO MAN 3</u>

<u>BONDED BY BLOOD</u>

<u>SHORTY GOT A THUG</u>

<u>THUGS CRY</u>

<u>THUGS CRY 2</u>

<u>THUGS CRY 3</u>

<u>TRUST NO BITCH</u>

<u>TRUST NO BITCH 2</u>

<u>TRUST NO BITCH 3</u>

<u>TIL MY CASKET DROPS</u>

<u>RESTRAINING ORDER</u>

<u>RESTRAINING ORDER 2</u>

<u>IN LOVE WITH A CONVICT</u>

<u>Coming Soon</u>

BONDED BY BLOOD 2

BOW DOWN TO MY GANGSTA

Raised as a Goon 2

Made in the USA
Monee, IL
14 November 2024

70136294R00108